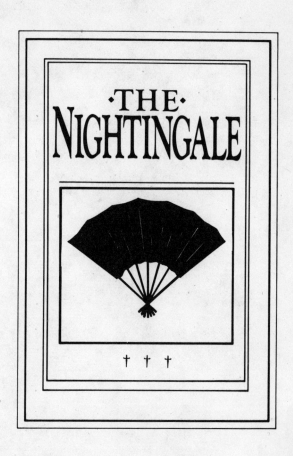

·THE·
NIGHTINGALE

† † †

·THE· NIGHTINGALE

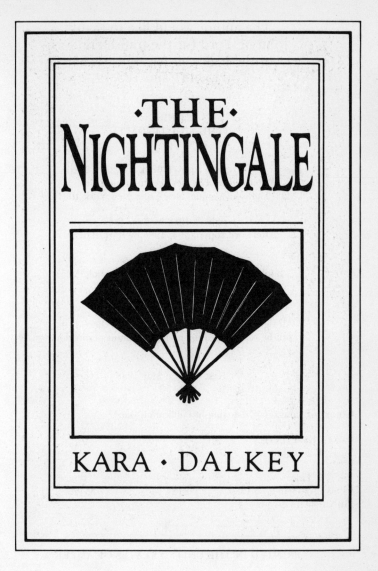

KARA · DALKEY

† † †

ACE BOOKS, NEW YORK

The author would like to thank
John M. Ford for the transliterations
of the haiku on pages 1, 51, 85,
113, 141 and 183.

UGUISU
(THE NIGHTINGALE)

An Ace Book
Published by The Berkley Publishing Group
200 Madison Avenue, New York, New York 10016

Book design by Thomas Canty and Arnold Vila.

† † †

First Edition: May 1988

Library of Congress Cataloging-in-Publication Data

Dalkey, Kara, 1953-
        The nightingale.

        I. Title.
PS3554.A433N54   1988   813'. 54   87-35126
ISBN 0-441-57973-6

† †

PRINTED IN THE UNITED STATES OF AMERICA

10 9 8 7 6 5 4 3 2 1

◆ ALSO BY KARA DALKEY ◆

The Curse of Sagamore (1986)

INTRODUCTION

◆ FAIRY TALES ◆

There is no satisfactory equivalent to the German word *märchen*, tales of magic and wonder such as those collected by the Brothers Grimm: *Rapunzel, Hansel & Gretel, Rumpelstiltskin, The Six Swans* and other such familiar stories. We call them fairy tales, although none of the above stories actually contains a creature called a "fairy". They do contain those ingredients most familiar to us in fairy tales: magic and enchantment, spells and curses, witches and trolls, and protagonists who defeat overwhelming odds to triumph over evil. J.R.R. Tolkien, in his classic essay on Fairy Stories, offers the definition that these are not in particular tales about fairies or elves, but rather of the land of Faerie: "the Perilous Realm itself, and the air that blows in the country. I will not attempt to define that directly," he goes on, "for it cannot be done. Faerie cannot be caught in a net of words; for it is one of its qualities to be indescribable, though not imperceptible."

Fairy tales were originally created for an adult audience. The tales collected in the German countryside and set to paper by the Brothers Grimm (wherein a Queen orders her stepdaughter, Snow White, killed and her heart served "boiled and salted for my dinner" and a peasant girl must cut off her own feet lest the Red Shoes, of which she has been so vain, keep her dancing night and day until she dances herself to death) were published for an adult readership, popular in the age of Göethe and Schiller, among the German Romantic poets. Charles Perrault's spare and moralistic tales (such as Little Red Riding Hood who, in the original Perrault telling, gets eaten by the wolf in the end for having the ill sense to talk to strangers in the wood) was written for the court of Louis XIV; Madame d'Aulnoy (author of *The White Cat*) and Madame Leprince de Beaumont (author of *Beauty and the Beast*) also wrote for the French aristocracy. In England, fairy stories and heroic legends were popularized through Mallory's Arthur, Shakespeare's Puck and Ariel, Spenser's Faerie Queene.

With the Age of Enlightenment and the growing emphasis on rational and scientific modes of thought, along with the rise in fashion of novels of social realism in the Nineteenth Century, literary fantasy went out of vogue and those stories of magic, enchantment, heroic quests and courtly romance that form a cultural heritage thousands of years old, dating back to the oldest written epics and further still to tales spoken around the hearthfire, came to be seen as fit only for children, relegated to the nursery like, Professor Tolkien points out, "shabby or old fashioned furniture . . . primarily because the adults do not want it, and do not mind if it is misused."

And misused the stories have been, in some cases altered so greatly to make them suitable for Victorian children that the original tales were all but forgotten. Andrew Lang's *Tam Lin*, printed in the colored Fairy Books series, tells the story of little Janet whose playmate is stolen away by the fairy folk—ignoring the original, darker tale of seduction and human sacrifice to the Lord of Hell, as the heroine, pregnant with Tam Lin's child, battles the Fairy Queen for her lover's life. Walt Disney's "Sleeping Beauty" bears only a little resemblance to Straparola's *Sleeping Beauty of the Wood,* published in Venice in the Sixteenth Century, in which the enchanted princess is impregnated as she sleeps. The Little Golden Book version of the *Arabian Nights* resembles not at all the violent and sensual tales recounted by Scheherazade in *One Thousand and One Nights* so that the King of Kings won't take her virginity and her life.

The wealth of material from myth and folklore at the disposal of the story-teller (or modern fantasy novelist) has been described as a giant cauldron of soup into which each generation throws new bits of fancy and history, new imaginings, new ideas, to simmer along with the old. The story-teller is the cook who serves up the common ingredients in his or her own individual way, to suit the tastes of a new audience. Each generation has its cooks, its Hans Christian Andersen or Charles Perrault, spinning magical tales for those who will listen—even amid the Industrial Revolution of the Nineteenth Century or the technological revolution of our own. In the last century, George MacDonald, William Morris, Christina Rossetti, and Oscar Wilde, among others, turned their hands to fairy stories; at the turn of the century lavish fairy tale collections were produced, a showcase for the art of Arthur Rackham, Edmund Dulac, Kay Nielson, the Robinson Brothers—published as children's books, yet often found gracing adult salons.

In the early part of the Twentieth Century Lord Dunsany, G.K. Chesterton, C.S. Lewis, T.H. White, J.R.R. Tolkien—to name but a few—created classic tales of fantasy; while more recently we've seen the growing popularity of books published under the category title "Adult Fantasy"—as well as works published in the literary mainstream that could easily go under that heading: John Barth's *Chimera,* John Gardner's *Grendel,* Joyce Carol Oates' *Bellefleur,* Sylvia Townsend Warner's *Kingdoms of Elfin,* Mark Helprin's *Winter's Tale,* and the works of South American writers such as Gabriel García Márquez and Miquel Angè Asturias.

It is not surprising that modern readers or writers should occasionally turn to fairy tales. The fantasy story or novel differs from novels of social realism in that it is free to portray the world in bright, primary colors, a dream-world half remembered from the stories of childhood when all the world was bright and strange, a fiction unembarrassed to tackle the large themes of Good and Evil, Honor and Betrayal, Love and Hate. Susan Cooper, who won the Newbery Medal for her fantasy novel *The Grey King,* makes this comment about the desire to write fantasy: "In the 'Poetics' Aristotle said, 'A likely impossibility is always preferable to an unconvincing possibility.' I think those of us who write fantasy are dedicated to making impossible things seem likely, making dreams seem real. We are somewhere between the Impressionist and abstract painters. Our writing is haunted by those parts of our experience which we do not understand, or even consciously remember. And if you, child or adult, are drawn to our work, your response comes from that same shadowy land."

All Adult Fantasy stories draw in a greater or lesser degree from traditional tales and legends. Some writers consciously acknowledge that material, such as J.R.R. Tolkien's use of themes and imagery from the Icelandic Eddas and the German Niebelungenlied in *The Lord of the Rings* or Evangeline Walton's reworking of the stories from the Welsh Mabinogion in *The Island of the Mighty*. Some authors use the language and symbols of old tales to create new ones, such as the stories collected in Jane Yolen's *Tales of Wonder,* or Patricia McKillip's *The Forgotten Beasts of Eld.* And others, like Robin McKinley in *Beauty* or Angela Carter in *The Bloody Chamber* (and the movie "The Company of Wolves" derived from a story in that collection) base their stories directly on old tales, breathing new life into them, and presenting them to the modern reader.

The Fairy Tales series, originally created by Armadillo Press and published by Ace Books, presents new novels of the latter sort—novels directly based on traditional fairy tales. Each novel in the series is firmly based on a specific, often familiar, tale—yet each author is free to use that tale as he or she pleases, showing the diverse ways a modern story-teller can approach traditional material.

The novel you hold in your hands is a fantasy retelling of Hans Christian Andersen's *The Nightingale*. Others in the series include *The Sun, the Moon, and the Stars,* which makes use of a Hungarian fairy tale in a contemporary setting, and *Jack, the Giant-killer,* in which the Faery Court lurks in the shadows of modern-day Ottawa. Fantasy and horror by some of the most talented writers in these two fields, retelling the world's most beloved tales, in editions lovingly designed—as all good Fairy Tale books should be. We hope you'll enjoy them.

From ancient times,
The plum tree is her resting place
The nightingale

—Onitsura

† † †

PROLOGUE

This story, esteemed reader, took place in ancient times. Do not ask precisely when, for it was oh so long ago. Before the Minamoto clan drove the Taira into the sea. Before shogun and samurai ruled the land. Before a pious woman created Kabuki dances. Before and before.

It was a time of gentleness, esteemed reader, and nobility. A time when the favorite pastimes of the Imperial Court were the writing of poetry and the viewing of the moon over Heian Kyo. This, then, is when and where this story took place.

It is not a story of war, esteemed reader, though there is conflict in it. It is not a romance, though there is love in it. It is not about court intrigue, though, Amida preserve us, it has enough of that. It is a story of life and learning, and wondrous things. It is a journey from foolishness to wisdom, from sorrow to joy.

If my humble efforts are successful, esteemed reader, it will entertain you. If my karma is great and Buddha smiles on me, it may enlighten you. If I am destined for a place in Heaven, you will wish to read it again.

Autumn

秋

Once words are said,
They leave a frost on the lips,
A breath of autumn wind.
                    —*Bashō*

THE FLUTE IN THE FIRE

THE COOL AUTUMN WIND whispered warnings to Uguisu as she threw more wood on the bonfire. The flames flickered higher and a sharp tang filled her nose as a too-green bough steamed in the blaze. Uguisu coughed softly and set out the torches of peeled hemp that she had lit from the bonfire. She held tightly onto the wide sleeves of her faded orange silk kimono as she worked. Even so, the wind threatened to fling an edge into the flames at any moment. Her very long, loose hair she had tucked underneath her kimono, to spare it from the ravages of wind and fire.

Once the hemp torches were set, Uguisu sat back on

◆1◆

her heels and sighed. It was the first night of U-Bon, Festival of the Dead, and an auspicious time for what Uguisu intended. It was said that this night spirits were permitted to return to earth for a period of three days. This night, the hemp torches were all that was necessary to summon the one Uguisu sought.

In the distance, Uguisu could hear the pounding of drums and rough voices of singers praising their ancestors. Though she sat by herself in the wild courtyard of an abandoned house in a most disreputable part of town, Uguisu felt no fear. Others would be too busy with their own celebrations to mind one more festival fire in their neighborhood.

And if a scoundrel should happen along and think me fair game, thought Uguisu, *well, it would scarcely matter.*

She carefully laid out before her the items she had brought for her expected visitor's approval: a cherry bough with a red silk cord dangling from it, a celadon bowl filled with water from the Kamo River, a knife whose sharp blade was wrapped in the purest white rice paper, and, in a small porcelain cup, the liver of a globefish. Once these were in place, Uguisu sat and watched the fire, waiting.

The smoke drifted upwards, shades of flame-tinted grey against a black night sky. As the wind gusted across the fire, the smoke twisted and spun like dancers on a fiery stage. Presently, a paleness appeared in the midst of the smoke, and Uguisu felt the hair on her neck stand on end. The paleness brightened into a blurry patch of light grey, then white. Lines spread across it, forming the wrinkled face of an old woman, whose white hair flowed behind her and upwards to mingle with the smoke. Two pale, gnarled hands appeared beneath the face. The left hand pointed at the objects Uguisu had set before the fire.

"Ah, Uguisu," the spirit said, with a voice like water spilled on hot coals, "This is an odd Festival offering you bring me."

Uguisu bowed deeply. "Oh Wise One, these are only symbols for what I truly offer you."

"Yes? And what might this true offering be?"

"I wish . . . I wish to offer you my miserable life!" Uguisu covered her face with her sleeves, hoping to stop the tears that threatened to flow.

"What! What is this you are saying?" said the spirit with a look of grave dismay.

"These things represent the ways in which I may end my joyless existence: the cord and the branch for hanging, the water for drowning, the knife for bloodletting, the fugu liver for poisoning. Tell me the method that is most proper in your sight, so that on the final day of the Festival I need no longer stay on this miserable earth. My spirit will, instead, follow you to Heaven."

"Foolish child! How can you say such things? How can you presume to know from what realm I come and where I would go? None of these methods pleases me. The offering of your life does not please me! Do you think I promised your mother that I would look after you and guide you, only to let you waste my efforts? Surely you must be mad, Uguisu. Could you truly wish to risk becoming a wandering ghost, or to suffer the Hell of Headlong Falling, because you are afraid of a few more tears brought on by this 'miserable' world?" The spirit sighed, and a gust of wind made the flames jump and sent dead leaves and ashes flying.

"So, Uguisu. What great calamity has forced you to consider shaming yourself and your family this way?"

From behind her sleeves, Uguisu replied, "My father has told me that there is no chance that I can marry the one I love—Niwa no Takenoko—and I must break with him. I am never to be with him again!"

"One could fill the sea with the tears of separated lovers, Uguisu. It is merely heartache that causes you to seek death in this miserable place?"

"If the gaudy pheasant may pine for its mate, may not the drab Uguisu feel loss too? If death finds me in this place, I do not care. Perhaps it might have worth, causing my father to ponder his 'frugality' in choosing a home near here."

"Bringing guilt upon your father with your death? And making your death an act of vengeance as well as liberation? How uncharitable of you, Uguisu! Your father is looking out for your best interests. What sort of life would you have with a gardener's son? What honor would he bring to your family?"

"But my father is looking only after *his own* interests. Being a noble of the Fifth Rank is not enough for him. He wants me to marry a Fujiwara!"

"It is understandable that your father would want to ally his family with the most powerful clan in the empire."

"But the Fujiwara I would most likely wed is Hidoi, and he's skinny and ugly and has the manners of an ox!"

"Now who is being selfish?"

"I know it would enhance my family's rank, but I just couldn't bear it. I love Takenoko."

The spirit sighed. "If it will ease your tormented heart, Uguisu, I have no intention of wasting you on such a boor as Hidoi."

Uguisu peeped over her hands at the face floating in the smoke. "Truly?"

"Truly. I have far greater plans for you. I intend that you will catch the interest of the highest ones at Court."

"The highest!" Uguisu gasped. "That's impossible. What would they have to do with such a lowly one as I?"

"See how little you know? Have some faith in me, child." The spirit waved a hand and the cherry branch sprung into the air. Another wave and the knife leaped into the flames, the paper sheath crisping instantly to ash. The red silk cord came off the branch, and then the spirit was juggling the bough, the knife and the cord in the air. Faster and faster the objects spun until they were only a blur in the fire.

Uguisu blinked, unable to keep her eyes on the spinning shapes. But, in the space of a few breaths, the movement slowed and stopped. Between the spirit's hands there floated a beautiful flute carved from the cherrywood bough. The red silk cord was wrapped around each end to strengthen and adorn it.

"Take this," said the spirit, "and give it ritual ablutions with the water from the Kamo River. The *fugu* liver you may throw into the fire, as it is more dangerous than useful."

Uguisu did as she was told, saying, "It is a beautiful flute, Wise One. But why should it catch the eyes of the First Rank, who have so many splendid things?"

The spirit sighed once more. "It is not the flute that will catch their interest, but your playing of it. Practice with it every evening on the banks of the Kamo River, letting no one see you, and I promise you will soon be hearing from the Imperial Court."

"But what of my love for Takenoko? A flute will not help me forget him."

The spirit raised her eyes to Heaven a moment, then

closed them. "I have foreseen that Takenoko will have a place in your household in the palace."

"He will? What do you mean, 'have a place'?"

"Ladies of the court are known to choose lovers when they will. When you are a lady of the court, who knows what you may do?"

Uguisu stared at the spirit, wide-eyed. "There is hope for us then? And I may also bring my family better position?"

"Perhaps."

"Thank you, Wise One!" Uguisu pressed her forehead to the ground.

"Be off now! Your father and servants will be wondering where you are if you tarry too long. Do as I have instructed, and call to me again once you have achieved position at court so that I may advise you further."

"Yes, Wise One! Thank you!" Uguisu bowed several times as the face in the fire faded again to a grey blur and vanished in a billow of smoke.

Gathering her robes around her, Uguisu stood, clutching the flute tightly. She hurried into the cool dark streets, full of relief and hope. She headed home, a northeast wind blowing her hair across her face. The beating of her excited heart seemed to match the rhythm of the death-drums nearby. For their sound, she could scarcely hear the distant thunder of an approaching storm.

Of Kiri Leaves

In the heart of the Imperial Nine-Fold Enclosure, in the midst of the opulent splendor of the Seriyō Den, His Shining Majesty the Emperor sat in a room that was utterly bare. Holy tags of ivory adorned his black eboshi cap and his wide sleeves of white silk brocade. His handsome face stared into nothingness as he tried to weigh the sins he had amassed in his forty-one years. Yet all he could feel was loneliness.

In a pool of sunlight that flowed into the room from beneath the raised blinds, there lay a cat. She had long, golden fur and big yellow eyes that blinked at the Emperor. Stretching luxuriously, she rolled onto her back and gazed at His Majesty with expectation.

"I am sorry, Lady Hinata," said the Emperor solemnly. "I may not pet you today."

The cat mewed and rolled over again.

"Do not reproach me, my lady. This is a holy day of Imperial Abstinence. Do you not hear the priests chanting the Sutra of Great Wisdom? On this day I must not eat, drink, touch a woman, read poetry, play games of Go, or do anything else pleasant or distracting. This day I am to sit and reflect upon the path my life has taken, and take measure of my sins. I must set a pious example for my court." He finished with a haughty tilt of his chin and turned his head to gaze out at the garden.

Then his eyes flicked back to the cat and a gentle smile slowly grew on his lips. "But I doubt even the Amida could resist such eyes." The Emperor reached out and picked up the cat, setting her on his lap. She immediately began purring loudly and curled up in contentment as his Majesty stroked her fur.

The Emperor again gazed out, past the veranda to the portion of the garden he could see from where he sat. There stood a *kiri* tree, all but one of whose heart-shaped leaves had fallen into a pile of reds, golds and browns at its base. To the Emperor, the leaves seemed like a crowd of courtiers in bright Palace robes, bowing obeisance to their lord, the one remaining leaf.

"See there, Lady Hinata, that leaf upon the tree? There

am I. Lofty, yet alone." The thoughts in his mind began to form into a poem, when there came a sudden gust of wind. The lone leaf was whipped off the branch and spun through the air until it disappeared from the Emperor's sight.

His Majesty closed his eyes and sighed. Taking up brush and inkstone, he wrote upon a fan of yellow paper:

> "—Even the highest leaf
> May find itself tumbling
> in the autumn wind."

By the Imperial Kitchen

"Sake!" called Inner Guards Lieutenant Kuma, pounding the floor with one end of his archer's bow. "More sake, Katte-san!" He grinned at the morose young man sitting across the low table from him.

The young man did not seem cheered. Arms crossed on his chest, he said, "Drowning me in rice wine will not make me forget Uguisu, Kuma-san."

A pretty woman in a plain cotton kimono hurried, scowling, out of the kitchen. She brought to the table a bottle and a pair of small bowls. "Hush, if you please, Kuma-san!" she whispered with extreme annoyance. "You should not be here. If the Master of the Kitchens should hear that I served you here, I would be dismissed at once."

"Ah, fear not, Katte-san. I have former comrades who are Chamberlains. They would see that the Household Office gave you no trouble."

"Hah. Much your courtly friends would care about this lowly one. And your Captain, if he hears—"

"I am not on duty until the Hour of the Boar tonight,

Katte-san. You worry too much. Now be good and pour, will you? My friend Takenoko here has much need of consolation."

"He should not be here either," the kitchen maid muttered.

"Now, now, have some compassion, Katte-san. Who do you think provides the blossoms from the garden for my love notes to you?"

The kitchen maid flushed and hurried away without another word.

"Ah, now there's a real woman, Takenoko. Did you see how strong she is? Not like those willow maidens of the court, who faint at the thought of anything more strenuous than lifting a writing brush or plucking a *koto* string. Yes, that is what we should do, Takenoko. We should find another woman for you." *Although that may not be an easy task,* thought Kuma, noting Takenoko's wiry build and tanned face. *Most women at court like their men pale as the moon and nearly as round. As I have learned.* He rubbed his narrow, hirsute face ruefully.

"There is no other woman for me," said Takenoko. "Besides, if you like that one so much, why haven't you married her?"

"Oh, my family still has hopes that I will marry well. If I were to become a Chamberlain, or something . . . who knows." He quickly downed a bowlful of sake.

"Hmp. Just like Uguisu's father. Tell me, Kuma-san, why is rank such a big thing?"

"It is not a big thing. It is everything! You know, there is no problem you have that could not be solved by exerting a little ambition. Where can you go from your current position, eh? You can become an Imperial Gardener, like your father Niwa. Which is better than being an ordinary gardener, but what then? Nothing. You will work with your hands in the dirt all your life until you become bent and gnarled as the trees you care for."

Takenoko nodded slowly. "You are right, Kuma-san."

"Of course I'm right. But, now, there are other paths open to you that you do not yet see."

"What do you mean?"

"You could join the Imperial Guards, boy! There's a career with promise! There's always a place for a young, strong lad like you. After all, we've got to get some worthy recruits to balance out the weak, spoiled noble-man's sons we're always getting stuck with. I would vouch for you. Come, place your offerings on the altar of Hachiman!"

"Hachiman," murmured Takenoko, toying with his sake cup. "I wonder if the God of War knows that here at court the Ministry of War is the least respected of all the offices."

"Pheh! You've been eavesdropping on too much gossip. What do those weakling bureaucrats know? Besides, it's better than gardening. And certain ladies of the court do not harbor such prejudices."

"I thought you said court ladies weren't worthwhile."

"Well, not for marriage, no. But they're fine for a lonely night's entertainment. What say you? Shall I sign you up tonight?"

Takenoko shifted uncomfortably. "Naturally I will consider your kind offer, Kuma-san."

From his tone of voice Kuma could tell that Takenoko had no intention of following through on the offer. Kuma sighed. *Love rarely makes one reasonable.*

"Yes," Takenoko went on, "I must consider carefully upon what altar I will make my offerings." Sighing, the young man stood. "Well, Kuma, I fear I must return to my work. My poor old father needs help more than he used to, and I should go to him. Thank you for your friendly advice. I shall give it all the consideration it deserves. Please excuse me." Takenoko bowed quickly and, sliding the *shoji* aside, hurried away.

"Hmpf," muttered Kuma, "so much for doing good works for one's fellow man." He stood and stretched slowly. Walking to the door, he leaned against the frame and stared out at the overcast sky. He heard soft footsteps behind him, but he did not turn around.

"It will rain tonight, don't you think?" said Katte.

"Hmm."

"I have not been able to repair your straw rain cape, but then you have not brought it to me as you said you would. Which of us should be blamed if you catch your death of cold?"

The Guards Lieutenant turned and looked at her in surprise, painfully noting the caring in her eyes.

The kitchen maid lowered her gaze to the floor. "I think I shall leave my door open tonight. With the kitchen so close, it is nice to have the rain-freshened air coming in."

"Then perhaps I will walk by, on my rounds, to see that no thieves crawl through your open door."

"Perhaps. Yes. That would be nice." Katte smiled and bowed, then trotted back to the kitchen.

"Perhaps," Kuma whispered, watching her leave. Then, gathering his red guardsman's jacket tighter around him, he stepped out into the first drops of evening rain.

The Fujïwara

The slopes of Mt. Otoko were ablaze with autumn color. From the white pebbled courtyard of the Iwashimazu Shrine of Hachiman, a robust, grey-haired man in a flowing black court cloak surveyed the scene with quiet satisfaction. He was Fujiwara no Daimigi, Minister of the Right, chief of his clan, and the most powerful man in the empire. And in his hands he held a trembling, plump white dove.

"Peace, little one," he murmured to the dove. He was charmed by the way she reminded him of the Emperor, who also seemed to be squirming lately within the Fujiwaras' political grasp. "You are fortunate, little one. You I intend to set free."

He continued to hold the dove while the priests of the temple chanted the Supreme Sovereign Sutra. Other high nobles of the court assembled in the yard, each bearing a creature to be "liberated." Koi carp were released in the temple ponds and young deer were set loose to run in the forest.

Daimigi noted his young daughter's ornate carriage by the shrine's fence and hoped she had a good view of the ceremony. She so loved animals. *Enjoy the outing while you can, my dear. Soon you must take the place of your sister, the late Empress. And the wife of an emperor may not travel everywhere as she pleases. It seems a terrible burden to place on you when you are so young, but it is for the good of all. The Emperor has no heir and you must give him one . . . an heir of Fujiwara blood. You will understand when you are older.*

A priest in white robes and triangular hat approached the minister and bowed. "My lord, you are the last."

Daimigi nodded and savored for a few moments more the captive life within his hands. Then gracefully he tossed the dove into the sky. He watched her flight until she disappeared behind the red and gold treetops.

"My lord!" the priest beside him suddenly exclaimed. "Your sleeve, my lord!"

Daimigi looked and saw that the dove's talons had

scratched his right wrist. A trickle of blood had seeped into the sleeve edge of his white under-robe.

"A bad omen, my lord."

"No. A good omen. Hachiman should be pleased by a sacrifice of blood in his shrine, don't you think?"

"As you say, my lord."

"Quite so."

The Minister of The Imperial Grounds

Uguisu knelt behind the shoji door to her father's study and silently slid it shut behind her. Across the room, the Minister of the Imperial Grounds sat on a cushion, his back to Uguisu, reading a scroll of what appeared to be a list of names.

A list of posts soon to be vacant, no doubt, so he'll know what to request for the New Year's promotions. As her father had not seemed to notice her yet, she took a moment to look at him, since she rarely had the chance. As usual when in his presence, she felt a mixture of admiration and distrust. He was an impressive figure, with his tall, black cap of office and his green over-robe indicating nobility of the Fifth Rank. *Yet even now,* thought Uguisu, *he probably dreams of wearing the black robes of higher rank.*

Her father began to turn his head, and Uguisu quickly ducked behind a curtain screen.

"Ah, Uguisu. Finally beginning to act like a lady, I see," said the Minister.

Uguisu felt herself blush with embarrassment and was grateful for the *kicho* curtain between them. The cloth panels were faded and threadbare, and therefore not much of a barrier, but the kicho was nevertheless important as a symbol of rank. Ladies of quality were not supposed to be seen by any man, except a lover or husband. When Uguisu's family lived in the provinces, it had been less important. But now that her father was a minister, he had begun to insist on such things. *And I suppose when I go to court myself, I will spend the rest of my life surrounded by these little screens, or behind paper doors or bamboo blinds.* Uguisu sighed. "Yes, father. You wished to speak to me?"

"Indeed. It has been some time since we had a talk, and our last conversation was regrettably unpleasant."

"Yes, father."

"I would have spoken to you sooner, but your maid Tetsuda says that you spend several hours each day away from home, and she could not tell me where you were."

So that's what he's wondering about. "Yes, father. I have been told that if I am to eventually have a place at court I should apply myself to improving my talents. Every day, for the past month, I have been pursuing musical studies. I only go away from home because I want no one to hear how terrible I sound while I practice. When I am good enough, of course, it will not matter who hears me."

"It pleases me to hear you say this, Uguisu. Since we had our last talk, I have been worried about you. I am glad you have come to see the correct way of things. Of course I knew you could not be doing anything foolish such as seeing that gardener's boy on the sly."

"No, father."

"You could not because I hear he has left the city. But since you have had a change of heart, I doubt that is important to you."

Uguisu felt as if someone had struck her in the stomach and she pressed her face into her voluminous sleeves to stifle an exclamation. *Takenoko gone! With no word to me. What does it matter now if I become a court lady who can do as she pleases?*

"Speaking of young men, I happened to talk to Fuji-wara no Hidoi yesterday."

"Did you?" Uguisu murmured softly.

"Yes. He said he has heard fine things about you, and would like to get to know you better. He gave me a note to give to you." The Minister thrust a folded piece of orange paper, with a wilting chrysanthemum stuck in it, beneath Uguisu's curtain. "He seems quite taken with you. In fact, it would not surprise me if he comes to visit you tonight."

The suggestive tone of her father's voice made Uguisu's stomach twist.

"Of course, it would be the sheerest impoliteness not to respond to Hidoi's note. If you write a reply now, I will take it with me when I see his father, the Minister of the Right, this afternoon." He slid a red paper fan under the curtain, along with an inkstone and brush.

So that you can read my answer, and substitute a better one if you don't approve of what I write, no doubt. "Give me a moment, if you please, while I read Hidoi's poem."

"Of course. Take your time. I would not want your response to be ill-considered."

Reluctantly, Uguisu unfolded the orange paper, brushing away the wilted flower within it. Hidoi's poem read:

> "Though it is autumn, in dreams I see
> an uguisu on my plum tree
> and feel yearnings of spring."

Crude, thought Uguisu. *And clumsy. How very like him.* She struggled with her thoughts for some moments, trying to come up with an unencouraging reply, but one that her father would not censor.

At last she set her brush to paper:

"The uguisu also longs for spring,
To have the plum flowers for her fine kicho."

This she passed under the curtain to her father, saying,
"I trust you can find an appropriate plant to send with
this. Perhaps a paper plum flower would be nice."

"This is a . . . very modest reply, Uguisu."

"Yes, father. Since it is important now that I act like a
lady, I felt it was a proper response." She found it difficult to keep the irony from her voice, and she hoped her
father wouldn't notice.

"Er, yes, of course. Well, I shall see that it gets to Hidoi
straightaway."

As Uguisu returned to her rooms, she still was not sure
if her note would reach Hidoi unaltered, but she was
satisfied she had done the best she could. If her father
substituted a more passionate poem, or if Hidoi chose to
misinterpret what she wrote . . . Could the Wise One
help her if Hidoi did come for the night? She began to
think of some way to slip out and make offerings to her
guardian spirit.

Just then her maid, Tetsuda, hurried down the corridor to her. "Lady Uguisu! As I was cleaning your rooms
I found this on your sleeping mat, under your cloak."
Tetsuda handed Uguisu a folded piece of brown paper,
and Uguisu felt something like a twig wrapped inside it.
Another poem from Hidoi? Uguisu thought with dread. Nod-
ding thanks to her maid, Uguisu hurried into her room.
She curled up on a cushion and paused a moment to
gather courage before opening the note.

But when she finally did so, her heart gave a momentary leap of joy, for the calligraphy was Takenoko's rough
hand. The twig was cherrywood, completely bare, but

finely shaped and shining as if polished. Takenoko's poem read:

> "Leaves leave the garden, washed away
> by autumn rain
> Never again to see the blossom
> that once was so near."

So it is true. He has gone, thought Uguisu. As tears filled her eyes, she picked up brush and ink. Below his poem, she wrote a reply, though knowing he would never see it:

> "Bare is the garden,
> washed empty by autumn rain.
> So, too, is my heart."

Mountain Path

Through the morning mist, Takenoko struggled up the mountain path. Ahead, up the slope beyond the low clouds, lay the Shingon Temple of Ninna-ji. Pine branches seemed to reach out and catch on his sleeve, as if trying to detain him.

Takenoko paused to catch his breath at a bend in the path. He looked back at the city of Heian Kyo in the valley below. He could see why poets often called it the "City of Purple Hills and Crystal Streams." Seen through the mountain mist, it was like a scene from a dream.

In time, will I think my life there was a dream? How can I leave such beauty for drab monk's robes and endless prayer? But he answered himself immediately. *There is no longer a life for me in that beauty. How could I stay and watch Uguisu marry another? Would I be better off grubbing in the palace gardens, scorned by those of higher rank? Or as a guardsman, viewed as an upstart and swaggering ruffian? No. The only life left for me is at the end of this path, beyond worldly suffering.*

His one regret was leaving his old father Niwa. Take-noko pulled out of his sleeve the note his father gave him when they parted and read it again:

"Usually it is the parent who aspires to Heaven before the child.

> If autumn winds should bear the seed to Heaven,
> what cause does this old willow have to weep?"

Takenoko looked back at the city and said,

> "I see my home behind me as I wonder,
> do trees hurt so when pulled up from their roots?"

He turned to go on and tripped on a rock, falling sprawled in the weeds beside the path. As he started to rise, he saw a small face peering at him through the underbrush. He was startled a moment, then realized the face was made of stone.

Sitting up, Takenoko cleared away some of the weeds and discovered a small stone Bodhisattva. Inscribed on its pedestal was the name "Aizen-myō."

Gazing at the statue, Takenoko wondered if its kami had stopped him for some reason.

A faint voice in his mind said, "To rise on the path to Heaven, first you must remove the rocks from your shoes."

Looking down, Takenoko thought, *But there are no rocks in my shoes.* Then he saw his father's note crumpled in his left hand, and understood. Sadly, Takenoko placed the note on the lap of the stone bodhisattva. Then he bowed three times and continued on his way.

Ladies of the Court

"Konnichi-wa, Shonasaki!"

"Konnichi-wa, Kitsune, Nikao. Has the rain driven you out of the Seriyō Den?"

"You could say that. The boredom certainly has. This wing of the palace tends to be warmer and cheerier. We came to hear some of your poems to relieve our melancholy."

The two ladies found cushions and seated themselves. Kitsune smiled, revealing a most fashionable set of dark-stained teeth. Her raven hair flowed like a river over her shoulders and down her back. Nikao was plumper, but she had a pleasing pale complexion and her eyes were like fine, narrow brushstrokes.

"I am afraid you two have chosen the wrong day to request poetry," said Shonasaki. "I haven't been able to write a thing all morning. My head feels completely empty."

"Why not write a poem about emptiness, then?" said Kitsune.

"Don't be silly," said Nikao. "One can't write a poem about nothing."

"I understand there are priests who compose sutras to it all the time," said Kutsune.

"Well," Shonasaki put in, "priests are surely better suited to exploring Nirvana than I. So far as I can tell, *this* is the only proper poem about nothing." She pushed forward a blank sheet of white rice paper.

"Ah, but that is not nothing, at all!" said Kitsune. "Look closer. There are grains and fibers in a delicate interweaving. This page is hardly empty."

"It seems there is a poem in that somewhere," said Nikao.

"Perhaps," conceded Shonasaki, "but I think Kitsune

should write it, since it's her idea and I wouldn't express it as well. Come now, there must be interesting things going on around the Emperor, where you are staying. Out here in the Plum Pavilion we only hear bits and snatches of gossip. Tell me what has been happening. Perhaps I can find a poem in that."

"Well," said Kitsune, "there really isn't much to say. Though it's been months since His Majesty came out of mourning for the dear late empress, things still seem dreary. His Majesty almost never visits his other ladies. And when he does, it's only to talk about old times."

"The seasons may be partly to blame," said Nikao. "Autumn is always a melancholy time, and this autumn seems drearier than usual. All this rain! No doubt it hasn't helped cheer His Majesty."

"A puddle of autumn rain," murmured Shonasaki, "A mirror of Our Majesty's heart."

"That sounds nice," said Nikao. "There, you have a poem."

"Almost," said Shonasaki, "almost. But the syllables just won't fall right." She sighed in frustration. "Keep talking, Kitsune. There must be something else to inspire me."

"Well, as I was saying, His Majesty doesn't spend much time with anyone . . . except that stupid cat of his."

"Lady Hinata?" Nikao said, surprised. "Why do you malign her? She's such a pretty cat, so sweet and gentle."

"Hah. You haven't found her sleeping on your favorite Chinese coat, shedding all over it."

Suddenly Shonasaki sat up and cried "Aha! That's it!" She grabbed a brush and wrote:

> "Ah, whose coat is this?
> The cat has given me hers,
> For the use of mine."

Nikao giggled when she read it. Kitsune said, "I don't think it's very funny."

"But at least I finally wrote one," said Shonasaki. "It seems I'm inspired by amusing things today. Tell me something you do find funny, and I might write a better one."

"Well, let's see . . . Ah! We did hear one amusing bit of gossip. One of the Inner Guards told us that last night Fujiwara no Hidoi, the son of the Minister of the Right, set out in his carriage to visit someone. But there had been so much rain that his carriage bogged down in the mud just outside the palace gate. This made Hidoi angry and he got out of the carriage and whipped the ox. But the ox became frightened and scrabbled in the mud, becoming mired itself. So Hidoi went about whipping his attendants who were trying to push the cart. This didn't help at all, and Hidoi strode about in such anger that he slipped and fell in the mud himself, soiling his beautiful court cloak. Hidoi then exclaimed that it was all a bad omen and that he should not have gone out at all that night. So he rushed back to his quarters and locked himself away, and has not been seen since. It is said he is serving a day of abstinence today as penance."

"More likely he's just ashamed to show his face for fear of ridicule," said Nikao.

"Do you know who he might have been going to visit?" asked Shonasaki.

"Well, there's a rumor that it might have been Uguisu, the daughter of the Minister of the Imperial Grounds," said Kitsune.

"Uguisu?" said Nikao. "That little thing? I imagine she's pleasant enough, but from what I've heard, she has little to recommend her. They say she hasn't even shaved her eyebrows. And her teeth are still a common white."

"But she's young," said Shonasaki, "and from the provinces. She hasn't spent any time at court, so she can't be expected to follow all the fashions."

"If she had a mother or aunt to look after her, she might be better informed," said Kitsune. "Why hasn't she been sent to court? Her father is an important minister, after all."

"No one even knows about her mother's family," said Nikao, "so they must be so lowly as to give her no backing whatsoever. Though her father long ago offered her as a lady-in-waiting to the court, no one has hired her because of this."

"Oh. Is that the reason?" said Shonasaki. "Poor Uguisu. Well, Hidoi must see something in her, surely."

"Yes," said Kitsune, "she's the only one who would have him."

All three ladies erupted in giggles at this. Footsteps on the veranda outside their blinds stopped and there came the voice of a male courtier.

> "What wind of fortune
> Brings sound of carefree laughter,
> On gales of autumn?"

The ladies put sleeves to their mouths with embarrassed delight. "You're the cleverest of us, Shonasaki," Kitsune whispered. "You must answer."

But she could only say:

> "The winds of fortune,
> May bring bad omens.
> We spoke of you, sir.

"Now do please hurry along, or we shan't be able to talk anymore."

The courtier outside chuckled and replied:

> "The winds of fortune
> are capricious breezes. I go
> Before I am drenched."

His footsteps passed on and the ladies sighed and laughed some more. "I think that was Fujiwara no Kazenatsu," said Kitsune. "I hear he's quite handsome, as well as elegant."

"Kazenatsu? Appropriate of him to speak of the winds, then," observed Shonasaki.

"He's a 'summer wind' indeed," said Nikao. "He certainly added some warmth to our gathering."

Kitsune shivered, causing her dark blue over-robe to ripple like a mountain stream. "Speaking of winds, I do feel a cold draft coming in. Can your blinds be secured more firmly?"

"I'll see," said Shonasaki, getting up and going to the veranda. As she tightened the fastening on the blinds, she saw a few snowflakes tumbling down through a grey sky.

"Snow so soon," she murmured. Hastily returning to her companions, she said, "It will be a cold winter this year, don't you think?"

WinteR

Cold winds from the river
Carve stone like steel knives
Beneath the winter moon.
                    —Bashō

ON THE BANKS OF THE KAMO

KATTE PULLED HER OLD, faded silk jacket tighter around her shoulders as she hurried across the snow. She was grateful that her wooden clogs were just tall enough to keep her stockinged feet from getting soaked. Katte did not like leaving the warmth of the kitchens on such a cold day, but there was no more ginseng root in the store-rooms and her ailing mother had great need of its medicine. The old gardener, Niwa, had told Katte the nearest place ginseng grew was by the Kamo River which flowed not far from the palace grounds.

Katte paused at the top of the slope that led down to the Kamo, catching her breath at the beauty of the scene before her. A mist had risen off the river, pearlescent in the morning sunlight. Here and there, the sail of a fishing boat would come into view, then vanish in the mist. The tops and lower branches of pines, sparkling with frost, seemed as if floating in air. To her left and slightly behind her, Katte could see the pointed roofs and curving eaves of the palace revealed through the mist.

It's like a Chinese painting, she thought, shivering with delight as well as cold. She imagined she could faintly hear the high, sweet notes of a courtier's flute borne to her on the frosty breeze.

As Katte carefully picked her way through u-no-hana shrubs, she realized that the flute music was not her imagination. Though still faint, the sound became clearer as she moved along the river's edge. Katte found herself entranced by the rippling melody and, without thinking, began to seek its source.

Before long, the kitchen maid came to a large pine, whose lower boughs reached down to the ground. Within the curtain of pine branches, Katte could see a portion of elegant violet-grey sleeves and skirt. *What lady would play such beautiful music behind a kicho of pine boughs?*

Suddenly, the music stopped. "Who is there?" said a cultured voice.

"It is no one, Lady of the Pine Curtain. I am most sorry to have disturbed you." Katte gathered herself to leave.

"Wait," said the lady. "Come under the tree, where I might see you."

"Oh, no, my lady. There is no need for you to see such a wretched one as I."

"Don't be silly. You needn't fear. I'm not a kami. I'm not even highborn. Come here."

Slowly, Katte parted the pine boughs and crept inside. As she sat down on a soft bed of damp needles, she dared to glance at the lady and was surprised that she looked so young.

The lady smiled and nodded in greeting. "What is your name?"

"If it pleases you, my lady, this lowly one is called Katte."

"A kitchen maid? How interesting. Do you find your life . . . fulfilling?"

Katte blinked and paused a moment. "Naturally it pleases me to serve Our Majesty, the Emperor, in whatever small capacity I may. Although I have often wished . . ."

"Wished what?"

"Well, you will doubtless consider it beneath your interest, but I have often wished to manage an inn located in some lovely setting."

The lady laughed. "That is a more ambitious aspiration than I have ever had. And if you serve Our Majesty, then it must be that you work in the Imperial kitchens. Believe it or not, you have seen more of the palace than I."

"I am surprised, my lady. Your music, I'm sure, would grace the halls at court. I could not resist coming to listen when I heard you."

"Thank you. I do hope to someday 'grace the halls at court.' But why were you wandering down this way at all?"

"My mother is ill, my lady. I came seeking ginseng root which, I am told, grows near here."

The young lady smiled. "Fortune must have let you hear my flute. As a matter of fact, there is some ginseng growing on the other side of this tree."

"There is?" Eagerly, Katte dug through the pine needles and found the roots she was looking for. "How wise you are, my lady, to have noticed these!"

"My mother knew many of the ancient medicines. I learned a little from her."

"How fortunate that you have a learned mother to teach you these things."

"My mother passed away many years ago, but I am grateful for what guidance she could give me."

"I am sorry to hear you have lost such a dear relative. I hope I do not lose my own so soon. I should hurry back to her. But could I please hear just one more tune from your flute, my lady?"

"Of course," said Uguisu, lifting the instrument once more to her lips.

The Chinese Book

The Emperor looked up as the Minister of the Right, Fujiwara no Daimigi, strode into the Imperial Audience Chamber.

It was the Hour of the Tiger, before dawn had risen, and the Minister showed every sign of having hurriedly dressed. His Majesty smiled to himself. *You would like to think me the puppet of your family,* thought the Emperor. *But I still have the power to make you damnably uncomfortable.* "Konnichi-wa, Daimigi-san."

"A good morning is it, your Majesty?" The Fujiwara gave a perfunctory bow before sitting. "Sometimes I think only the tiger loves this particular hour of darkness."

"Truly? I had learned that the Great Reform of my forebears stipulated this hour for the commencement of daily official business. Ah, how things have deteriorated since those noble, ancient times. But you should be pleased to know, Daimigi-san, that I would not have summoned you if I did not have an important reason." In truth, the Emperor was momentarily tempted to claim that he had changed his mind and send the Minister fuming home. But he could not yet risk enraging the head of the Fujiwara clan.

A calculating look came into the Minister's eyes. "Well, though it may seem unusual to begin the day before the dawn, there is no harm in yearning for the cherry blossom before spring, eh?"

Ah, that's why he thinks he's here. He thinks I wish to discuss marrying his daughter. "Do we speak of cherry blossoms or maiden flowers now? No matter. I do not think it appropriate to fuss over flowers not yet in season." *In other words, Daimigi-san, your little fourteen-year-old girl is too young for me.*

"But the most insignificant of buds, Your Majesty, may yet become the most beautiful of blossoms."

"Nonetheless, if one picks a bud too soon, there may be no bloom at all. But I did not ask you here to discuss gardening."

"Is it, then, the Day of Promotions that concerns you, Your Majesty? I can assure you that I have seen to all arrangements. There is no need for you to sully yourself with involvement in the pettiness of politics."

"You are, as always, too kind, Daimigi-san. I will admit to being curious about what arrangements are being made. I would like to know if gifts from me are needed and appropriate, and of what sort."

"Your Majesty's renowned generosity would be most appreciated, I am sure. But I do not have the list of arrangements with me. I left it in my office, where my clerks will be making copies of it today. I will have a copy delivered to you as soon as one is ready, if you wish."

You mean as soon as it is too late for me to do anything about it.

"That would be most thoughtful of you, Daimigi-san.

But I have digressed. I did not ask you here to discuss the New Year's promotions either." *Not directly, at least.*

The Fujiwara looked perplexed. "May I ask, then, what it is you do wish to discuss, Your Majesty?"

"Yes, Daimigi-san. It concerns this book you gave me some days ago." With the end of one finger he tapped the wooden cover of a tome on his lap.

"A . . . book, Your Majesty? Ah, would that be the notebook left me by the Chinese scholars?"

"The same. There is a passage here that disturbs me."

"Disturbs you, Your Majesty?"

"That is what I said."

"Of course, Your Majesty. I am most humbly sorry you are disturbed. I had thought it to be an innocuous work—merely a recording of the scholars' impressions of the capital during their visit. I thought you might find it amusing."

"And so I have, Daimigi-san. Except for this one passage."

"What is the offending portion, Your Majesty?"

"It is here, near the end, where it is written: '. . . So, in all, Heian Kyo is a most charming little city. But one experience we must note was the day we were boating on the Kamo River. We were near the grounds of the Imperial Palace when we heard on the wind a flautist playing the most exquisite music. We were all quite entranced by it, and agreed it was finer than any we had heard at court in Ch'ang-an. Later that day, we endeavored to discover the identity of the musician, but none we could ask could tell us. No doubt the Emperor of Nippon wishes to keep the flautist his own court secret.' And so on."

"I thought it a rather pleasant passage, Your Majesty."

"Did you? And do you know who this flautist is that the scholars write of?"

"Er, not exactly, my lord. We have many excellent musicians at court. It could have been any one of them."

"While I agree that many of our court musicians are excellent, this is the first time I have heard one described as better than those in the court of China. Don't you find it a little odd that I do not know who this excellent flautist is?"

"Perhaps the scholars exaggerated the musician's skill out of politeness."

"That is a tendency of diplomats. Scholars, I have noted, tend to do the opposite. I want this flautist found, Daimigi-san. Do any of these scholars remain in Heian Kyo?"

"Only one, my lord."

"Good. I want you to arrange a gathering of the best flautists in Heian Kyo at your mansion. Have the Chinese scholar, discreetly hidden, tell you which one is the one he heard by the Kamo River. Then have that flautist brought to me. Do not let on, however, that we do not know the musician's identity. Let the scholar think we are testing him."

"An excellent idea, Your Majesty. But is this matter so important that we must pursue it now? This is a very busy time, you know."

"I thought you said all arrangements had already been made for the promotions. And, yes, I consider it important. You have often said yourself, Daimigi-san, that the cultural life of the court should be my primary concern. Is it not an embarrassment for there to be such a fine musician heard by foreign visitors but unknown to me? And would it not be appropriate for this flautist to play at the New Year festivities?"

The Minister sighed. "I understand. It shall be as you request, Your Majesty." He bowed and turned to leave.

"Oh, one more thing, Daimigi-san. Should the scholar

not choose any of the musicians you invite, then I shall require a thorough search of the palace, perhaps the city also, to find the flautist. I want him in the Plum Pavillion by sunset tomorrow, or I fear I will have nothing better to do with my time than tinker with the list of promotions." The Emperor noted with satisfaction the annoyance that passed across the Minister's face.

"Of course, Your Majesty. It shall be as you say." The Minister bowed himself out of the room.

That should keep him busy for a while, thought the Emperor, closing the book in his hands with a firm snap. He called out to a lady-in-waiting behind the shoji. "You may send the guardsman in now."

There came the sound of movement and the rustling of silk, and the shoji slid aside. A handsome man wearing the stiff white trousers and red jacket of the Inner Palace Guard entered. He immediately kneeled and bowed, his head touching the floor. "You sent for me, Most August Majesty?"

"You are Guards Lieutenant Kuma?"

"That is so, Your Majesty."

"I understand you are a loyal and brave man, Kuma."

"This one is most pleased that you think so, Your Majesty."

"Excellent. I have a request of you, Kuma. I had heard you are currently serving in the Fujiwara palace, neh?"

"That is so, Your Majesty."

"Good. In the office of the Minister of the Right, you will find a scroll listing the arrangements for the promotions ceremony. I want you to take that scroll and replace it with this one." The Emperor pulled a scroll bound with a scarlet silk cord from beneath his cushions and handed it to the guardsman. "No one must see you do this. I cannot help you if you are caught. But you should have little interference if you go now and are swift about it."

"Yes, Your Majesty." The guardsman backed out of the room and silently hurried away.

The Emperor heard a "Prrow?" by his elbow, and saw Hinata sitting there. "Ah, Lady Hinata, have you been watching all this?" He scratched her ear, but she just stared at him.

"Do you disapprove of my subterfuge, Hinata-san? Surely you have lived in this palace long enough to see that the lives of all nobles are like a game of Go. So far I have been only a white stone on the board. Perhaps now I may become a player."

In the Minister's Office

Silent as snowfall, Kuma slipped down the corridor. The candle he held gave only a dim glow in the pre-dawn darkness. Suddenly a floorboard creaked and Kuma winced and froze in place. He cursed himself for forgetting that "singing boards" were often installed in palaces to warn of intruders.

Fortunately, he could hear in the distance the cries of outriders and chamberlains as the Minister set out into the city. *That should cover any noise I make.*

Kuma proceeded down the corridor until he reached an open doorway that led into the Office of the Right. Across the hall, faint lamplight glowed behind a closed shoji, but there was no silhouette on the translucent paper door. Kuma decided its occupant must be sleeping or absent.

He turned and entered the office. In the dim candle-light, Kuma saw several low tables on which there lay inkstones and brushes. At the far end of the room was an

L-shaped desk upon which lay a large scroll. Kuma carefully picked his way across to the desk. Beside the scroll was a note saying "Ten copies."

"This must be the one," murmured Kuma, and he quickly pulled the Emperor's scroll out of his sleeve and switched it with the other. He felt somewhat uncomfortable, having not been involved in intrigue like this before. But he could hardly disobey a request from the Emperor himself.

Kuma headed back to the doorway, relieved that his task was finished. At the doorway, he stopped in horror as he saw the shoji across the hall was open. In that room sat a boy of about fifteen in a blue robe with a folded book on his lap. He was staring at Kuma intently.

Kuma felt his throat go dry as he recognized the boy—he was Korimizu, Fumiwara no Daimigi's youngest son. For a couple of heartbeats, Kuma simply stared back. Then he said, "I was patrolling outside, when I thought I heard a disturbance in here. I came to see if all was well."

"And is all well, guardsman?" the boy asked in a calm tenor voice.

"Yes, my young lord. Nothing has been disturbed." Kuma bowed and tried to stride confidently down the hall, praying to whatever kami watched over him to give the Fujiwara lad a poor memory.

The Search

"Make way! Make way!"

The Minister of the Imperial Grounds was jolted awake as his carriage passed over the ground beam of the Fujiwara Palace's main gate. The shrill cries of his outriders brought him to awareness of where he was, and he chided himself for drifting off.

If only Daimigi-san didn't choose to do his business so cursedly early in the morning! Poets might write glowingly of sleeves dampened by morning dew, Netsubo thought, but on this wintry morn all he could wish for was more hours of sleep.

Another jolt and the ox-carriage stopped. The Grounds Minister peered out of the carriage blinds, and saw an elegant garden of moss and evergreens glistening with new-fallen snow. As he unfolded himself and got out of the carriage, the outriders swept a path for him through the snow to the entrance of the mansion. Carrying himself with as much dignity as he could muster, the Minister allowed himself to be guided to Daimigi's reception room.

It was with appreciation for the justice of fate that Netsubo noted that the Fujiwara, too, looked ill-prepared to greet the morning. His eyes were red-rimmed and he rubbed them often with his fingertips. Even Daimigi's eboshi cap sat slightly askew on his head.

"A glorious good morning, Daimigi-san." Netsubo bowed low.

"Is that what it is, Netsubo-san? I am glad someone has reason to think so."

Bad news, then, eh? thought the Grounds Minister.

After several half-hearted inquiries into the well-being of Netsubo's family, Daimigi abruptly said, "There is a matter of some urgency that I believe falls under the jurisdiction of your office."

"I am, as always, prepared to serve."

"Excellent. I shall be counting on you. It concerns a musician, a flautist to be exact, who is said to be more skilled than any in the Imperial Court of China."

"Indeed?"

"Some scholars from that country noticed the playing of this musician during their visit and remarked upon it.

The unfortunate thing is that our Emperor does not know who this musician is."

"Would it not be a simple matter for you to bring this fellow to court?"

"Ah, but I do not know who he is."

"Could not one of the scholars point out this musician to you?"

"So I had hoped, last night. On Imperial order, I gathered the best flautists in Heian Kyo here, to be heard by the scholar. Alas, the fellow had the nerve to claim, after listening to each, that the flautist he had heard was a hundred times better."

"This is indeed a mystery, Daimigi-san. But what has this to do with my office?"

"His Majesty wishes to have this musician presented to him by sunset this evening. The scholars have said that the flautist was heard along the Kamo River, near the palace grounds. I want you, as minister of said grounds, to find this musician. You must ask everyone who might have heard him, from the highest to the lowest. Search thoroughly until this person is found. There must be someone who has heard him. I leave it in your hands."

Danger and opportunity, thought the Grounds Minister. *If I succeed, there is much to be gained. And the New Year's promotions are not far off. If I fail—*

"I shall send my son Hidoi with you to assist you, since you have been kind enough to show interest in him lately. He has been finding the winter months tedious and is in need of diversion. Ah, here he comes."

The tromping of careless footsteps could be heard well before a short, angular young man entered the room. "Morning, Father. Minister." The boy gave a perfunctory bow to each and sat none-too-gracefully on a cushion, sleepily rubbing one bony cheek.

More danger and opportunity, thought Netsubo. *I may get the chance to speak to him again about my daughter. Perhaps he is a bit ungainly now, but with maturity and position he will become impressive. I can't see why Uguisu does not show more interest in him. I must be certain not to look foolish in his sight.*

Not looking foolish was a task that became more difficult as the day wore on. Netsubo and Hidoi spent hours wandering the Imperial Palace grounds, asking clerks and chamberlains, ladies and waiting-maids about the unknown musician. None seemed to know who the person was. None had heard the playing of a flute by the Kamo River. By the middle of the Hour of the Sheep, the two sat wearily on a veranda, fanning themselves despite the cold.

Netsubo saw one of the Inner Palace Guards strolling by. "You! You there! Come here!"

The guardsman looked up, startled and wary, then approached the veranda.

"What is your name, Guardsman?"

"Kuma, if it please Your Lordship."

"Your name does not impress me one way or another, Kuma-san. How can you think to be standing idle, when there is work to be done?"

"Work, Your Lordship? If you have a task for me—"

"I most certainly do. You are to tell all the men in the Guard to search the palace for anyone who knows of the Flautist of the Kamo River. I place you personally in charge. There will be severe penalties if you fail in this. Now be off!"

The guardsman's eyes widened, and he bowed quickly. "Yes, Your Lordship." He ran towards the nearest guard station, shouting orders.

"There, now, Hidoi-san. That is the proper way to handle such business. Let others wear their clogs off, eh?"

The boy grinned back at the Minister, eyes bulging in his wide face.

Yes, a pleasant lad. Perhaps now is the time to broach another subject. "I am sorry that you have not had the opportunity to visit us, Hidoi-san. Uguisu has been asking about you and seems quite anxious to meet you. You know you are always welcome whenever you should choose to come by."

Hidoi blinked in surprise. "I have tried, sir! Believe me, I am aware of your kind invitation and I have not meant to slight you or your daughter. But I must say in all honesty, sir, that I believe a meeting between Uguisu and myself is ill-omened. The first time I tried to visit, my carriage became hopelessly mired in mud. The second time, no sooner had I left the palace than my sleeves caught on a passing branch, tearing my robes wide open. The third time, there was a procession of pilgrims returning from the Inari Shrine and my carriage was caught in such traffic that it took me hours to extricate myself. The fourth and last time I wished to visit, my father's Master Divinator claimed that your house lay in an unlucky direction and I had to go to someone else's house entirely!"

"It seems to me, Hidoi-san, that you have merely had a run of bad luck, not that my daughter is ill-omened."

"I'm sorry. I meant no offense, sir. Believe me, I'd like nothing better than to visit your daughter. Whenever I try to visit any of the ladies here at court, they always run away shrieking and making horrible faces. And the few I catch never respond to my next-morning poems. It's been quite lonely, I tell you." Hidoi sniffed, either from cold or self-pity, and wiped his nose on his sleeve.

Netsubo turned his face away. *He is a Fujiwara,* he

reminded himself. *He will grow to be worthy one day.* "Ants do not recognise the beauty of the blossom they crawl over. Fear not, my young lord, you will someday receive the respect you deserve. My Uguisu is already aware of your fine qualities. Perhaps this has simply been a busy time for you. We might arrange, perhaps, a meeting closer to the New Year?"

"That sounds like a good idea. You are most kind, sir, to take such interest in me."

"Not at all."

Just then, the blind behind them was raised and Fujiwara no Korimizu joined them on the veranda. Netsubo knew little about Daimigi's youngest son, except that he was a serious, scholarly boy.

"Father wishes to know if you've made any progress," said Korimizu.

"No," said Hidoi. "Say, what's that? Your pillow book?" Hidoi grabbed the book from Korimizu's hands, allowing the folded pages to flop out.

"Hey! Be careful, will you?" said Korimizu.

Hidoi ignored him and opened the wooden cover. " 'The Sutra of Filial Piety'? Feh. How dull." He gathered the paper together and tossed the mess back in Korimizu's lap. As Korimizu sadly refolded the pages, Hidoi turned to Netsubo and said, "People say it is a blessing to have brothers. Not for me. Kazenatsu knows plenty of interesting women, but he won't share them with me. He doesn't even want me around when he goes visiting. And 'Ice Water' here only likes to stick his nose in books."

Korimizu gave Hidoi an offended look and said,

"The maiden flowers do not interest
One who knows the glory of the lotus."

And Hidoi responded,

"The flower that grows in musty books is doomed
To watch the dew dry on his withered stem."

As Netsubo winced at the possible crude interpretations on Hidoi's poem, a cluster of young women appeared across the garden from where they sat. The ladies wore cloaks of bright red and white, and covered their faces with crimson fans or many-layered sleeves. "Here, flautist, flautist!" they called. "Come out, come out, wherever you are!" They laughed and giggled as they spilled into the garden. Running about in the powdery snow, like early plum blossoms tossed about by a gale, they pretended to search under rocks and behind trees.

"You, there!" Netsubo called sternly, waving his ivory baton of office at the ladies. "This is serious business! It is not one of your foolish games!"

The ladies suddenly noticed him and giggled louder with embarrassment and surprise. One of them pointed at the young Fujiwaras and said, "A summer frog beside a frozen pond. How unseasonal!"

This was greeted with more laughter by the other girls.

"If you cannot be proper and civil, then be off with you!" shouted the Grounds Minister. "Begone!"

"If he doesn't want our help, let's not bother," said one of the girls. "Come, let's go build a snow mountain in the Seriyō-Gardens! I'm sure we could make one higher than has ever been made!" Together the ladies fluttered away, incongruous butterflies against a snowy background.

Hidoi watched them go with an expression of sadness. Korimizu gathered up his book and disappeared behind the blinds. The garden seemed suddenly colder and Netsubo and Hidoi sat for a while in silence.

Presently, Hidoi pointed out something moving behind a tree. "Look, there's old Niwa. We should ask him what he knows."

"The gardener? Phaugh, what could he possibly tell us?"

"Oh, he knows a lot about what goes on at Court. They say the very leaves of the trees are his ears, he knows so much gossip. Hoi! Niwa-san! Come here!"

A small figure, as brown as the tree-trunk he stood behind, peered out at them. "Eh? What's that? Did someone call for old Niwa?"

"The leaves are his ears indeed," muttered the Grounds Minister.

"Don't be fooled," said Hidoi. "He's sharper than he lets on. Yes, Niwa-san! Come talk to us."

Slowly, a knobby gnome of a man hobbled out from behind the tree and came toward them. At a respectful distance, he stopped and bowed, then looked up, his eyes merely two more wrinkles in a deeply seamed face. "How can Niwa help you, my Lords? It is a poor time of year for poem-blossoms, but there are pine twigs a-plenty and the daikon is coming up fine."

Netsubo thought, *To think that my daughter loved the son of this . . . creature. Yes, she will definitely be better off with Hidoi.* "Nothing like that, Niwa. We are asking everyone if they have heard an excellent flautist playing near the Kamo River, and if they know who this person is. I don't suppose you have heard anything useful to us."

Niwa fingered his sparse grey beard and looked up in thought. "Kamo . . . Kamo," he murmured.

Netsubo sighed and looked away. *Why did we bother—*

"Why, yes," said Niwa, his dark eyes flicking towards the Minister, "I have heard someone speak of a flute player by the Kamo River."

"You did? Quick, man, tell us his name! Who spoke of the flautist?"

"Old Niwa will do better than that, my lords. Niwa will take you to her."

"Her?" Netsubo and Hidoi looked at each other. "What lady could we possibly have missed?" said the boy.

"Come, come, my lords," said Niwa, gesturing with one knobby arm. "She is this way." He hobbled off with surprising speed.

The Minister and the young Fujiwara got hastily to their feet and scuffled after the little gardener. As he led them through gardens and down hallways, curious courtiers and ladies-in-waiting followed behind, eager to see what was happening. Soon Hidoi, Niwa and the Minister found themselves at the head of a long, colorful parade of laughing people. The Minister tried to wave them away, saying, "This is serious business!" to no avail. Hidoi, to Netsubo's irritation, was enjoying himself immensely. Niwa, if he noticed those who followed at all, made no sign of it.

At last, the gardener led the procession into the Imperial Dining Room. It was currently empty, except for a kitchen maid who knelt wiping the polished wood floor. "Well, here we are," said Niwa.

Seeing no one of any consequence, the Minister turned angrily to Niwa and raised his hand to cuff the old man for tricking them into a useless chase.

"No, no!" cried Niwa, raising his arms to ward off blows. "She is here! Look!" The gardener hurried over to the kitchen maid and grasped her gently by the shoulders. "Katte-san, get up. These gentlemen here wish to speak to you."

The kitchen maid gasped and slowly stood. Shyly facing away, she said, "What do my lords wish of this lowly one?"

"Niwa-san says you have heard the excellent flautist who plays by the Kamo River," prompted Hidoi.

Katte glanced at Niwa who nodded at her encouragingly. "Yes, my lords. There is a lady who sits beneath a pine tree, on the riverbank, playing the most beautiful music this lowly one has ever heard."

"Who is she?" Netsubo demanded. "Tell us her name!"

"I have not presumed to ask her name, sir. I know her only as the Lady of the Pine Curtain."

Netsubo threw up his hands in exasperation. "You are nearly no help at all! How are we to find this nameless lady?"

"Please excuse me, my Lords, but she may be playing there now. This lowly one can lead you to her."

"Do so, immediately! And I tell you, if you lead us astray you will be scrubbing the palace latrines instead of the kitchen floors!"

So as the courtiers watched in wonder, the parade began anew, this time with the kitchen maid at its head. Out away from the palace she led them, toward the Kamo River. At the river's edge she stopped and looked about, listening.

"Well?" said the Grounds Minister.

"My Lord, I fear the voices of the others are too loud—"

"Silence!" the Minister bellowed at the nobles behind him. In a moment, they quieted until one could hear the whistling of the wind through the pine trees.

Hidoi frowned. "That doesn't sound like excellent music."

"No, my Lord. That is the wind. Please follow me."

Katte led them south along the river's edge until they came to a large pine, whose snow-covered boughs reached down to the ground. From behind the branches came exquisite music. It was soothing as the calls of evening birds, beguiling as the laughter of mountain streams, yet awe-inspiring as temple bells. The paraders stood smiling with amazement and joy.

Presently the music stopped, and Netsubo called out, "Lady of the Pine Curtain! Come out and show yourself to us! It is I, the Minister of the Imperial Grounds, who demands this!"

There was silence a moment. And then the pine boughs parted and a young woman, face modestly hidden behind her sleeves, emerged. "Good afternoon, father," she said. "Are you looking for me?"

In the Plum Pavillion

Moonlight flowed into the Plum Pavillion, a milky river of pale light. The blinds and shoji between the main room and the veranda had been raised and opened to welcome the radiance of the full moon. Small braziers of coals and paper lanterns were set among the nobles in the room and the ladies seated behind large screens, to give a little warmth and light. To Uguisu, seated behind a kicho of thin silk, the lights seemed like glowing stars, reflecting the night sky outside. In this setting she could easily understand why the Imperial Palace was poetically referred to as "heaven."

Nonetheless, despite the beauty around her, Uguisu felt uneasy. She was acutely aware that somewhere behind her curtain, amid the myriad perfumes and rustling silks, sat the Emperor himself, waiting for her to play. Discreet murmurs of cultured voices around her speculated softly on what she might look like, be like. Though she wore many layered kimonos and sat behind a kicho,

Uguisu did not feel nearly hidden enough. She held her hands over her own little brazier, wishing they would stop trembling.

Suddenly someone tugged on her sleeve. Her father, who sat just outside her kicho, hissed. "You must play, Uguisu! His Majesty is becoming impatient."

"Of course, father. I'm sorry." She raised the flute to her lips, fearing it might fall from her fingers she trembled so. But as the first notes spilled out, she felt her fear flow with them, and the music carried her far beyond her cares.

The flute sang of the beauty of the winter's full moon, sang lovingly of a gentle snowfall, with undertones that hinted at the buds of spring that lay beneath it. The flute sang on of the camaraderie of friends bringing warmth to a winter's evening, weaving in familiar strains of *saibara* in inventive ways. The flute sang of love sadly parted and love joyfully regained.

At last, Uguisu felt the music run down like a lantern of a departing friend receding in the distance. Reluctantly, she let it end and, with a sigh, set the flute down on her lap. Around her there was only silence.

Then there came excited murmurs of wonder. "Look at the Emperor!" people whispered to each other. "Look at the Emperor!"

Curiosity overcame Uguisu's sense of propriety, and she peeked out between two panels of her curtain. In the center of the room sat a handsome man, perhaps of forty years, dressed in magnificent white brocade, with under-robes of deep purple. And on his enraptured, noble face lay a glistening tear.

Uguisu gasped and pulled back the curtain, her heart pounding. Then came the Emperor's voice—she knew it could only be his voice—saying:

"The nightingale brings joyous rains from Heaven,
So long unshed. What shall they bring to her?"

"His Majesty wishes to reward you," her father whispered. "You must answer, but answer wisely. Much depends on your reply."

Uguisu felt her throat tighten and her tongue stick to the roof of her mouth. There was only one answer which felt right to her, though it would no doubt upset her father. In a soft tremulous voice she replied:

"The rains of Heaven nourish all the earth,
The nightingale finds this reward enough."

To her surprise, Uguisu heard whisperings appreciative of her response. "How elegantly restrained!" they said. "How gentle and ladylike!"

The Emperor said, "If my tears of happiness are your reward, then play on and you shall be many times repaid."

So Uguisu again raised up her flute and played long into the night, and no one noticed the cold of the winter wind.

New Year's Eve

"Hand me another bundle," said Kitsune as she finished filling another basket with brightly tasseled talismans for the Day of the Hare.

"Here you are," said Nikao, giving her more of the little sticks. "I am so excited! It was so dreary not having New Year celebrations last year. This New Year shall seem twice as fine!"

"Now that His Majesty is happy again, and no longer in

mourning," said Shonasaki, "the New Year shall dawn as bright as a new day."

Kitsune laughed. "His Majesty is apparently anticipating the dawn—they say the lamps have been burning late into the night in Seriyō Palace. I hear he is planning some surprises for tomorrow."

"More surprises!" said Nikao. "As if these past few days have not provided surprises enough."

"Indeed," said Shonasaki. "I shall never forget the look on the Grounds Minister's face when he discovered the flautist by the Kamo was his own daughter!"

"And he tried to be so stern during the search." Nikao took on an expression of mock severity and, brandishing a hare-stick, said, "This is serious business!"

All three ladies instantly dissolved into helpless laughter.

Kitsune, who recovered first, said, "Well, and who would have expected it of little Uguisu? She must have been hiding her skill behind a mountain to not be noticed for so long."

"Especially from her father," added Nikao, "though I suppose he has been busy with other things of late. Ah, but she played so beautifully that night!"

"It is surprising that she has chosen the flute as her instrument. I could understand a koto, or a biwa, but flute is a man's instrument."

"Should a young girl not be interested in playing upon a man's instrument?" said Shonasaki, one eyebrow arched.

Kitsune threw a cushion at her. "Oooh, you're horrid, Shonasaki!" She said, smiling despite her words.

"But delightfully horrid," added Nikao.

Suddenly there came from outside the sound of running feet and twanging bows. Nikao gasped with joy. "They're running the Demon Chase again!"

Kitsune moved toward the blinds. "Oh, I wish we could see it!"

"I sometimes wonder," said Shonasaki, "if the poor man in the demon mask ever gets hit by the arrows they fire at him."

"Don't be silly," said Kitsune, "I'm sure the guardsmen try to miss."

"Oh, I hope they chase all the evil spirits and demons of unhappiness from the palace!" said Nikao.

"There are no demons or evil spirits in the palace, Nikao," Kitsune chided. "The guardsmen and the iris balls see to that. And tomorrow the iris will be taken down and replaced with these sticks."

"And these sticks will stay up till the Iris Festival in summer," Shonasaki added.

"But if the talismans keep all demons and spirits out," said Nikao, "why do we have a Demon Chase the last night of the year?"

"To show any demons who might be watching what we'll do to them if they try to get in," said Kitsune.

"Speaking of watching demons," Shonasaki said mischievously, "I hear Kazenatsu was doing all he could to catch a glimpse of Uguisu while she was here."

"Don't say such things," said Kitsune, "or I shall become terribly jealous."

"Oh, you needn't lose hope for Kazenatsu," said Shonasaki. "He will have competition enough. There is a rumor that the Emperor himself will invite Uguisu to come to Court."

"He will?" said Nikao, shocked. "You don't think—"

"Don't be silly. She's much too common," said Kitsune. "He'll probably just install her as a lady-in-waiting to one of his lesser ladies and only bring her out when he wants a little music."

"Who can say?" said Shonasaki, staring absently at one corner of the room. Taking up a brush, she wrote on snow-white paper:

"A nightingale emerged from the snow.
A phoenix for the new year? What betides?"

Raising the brush, Shonasaki stared, dissatisfied, at her work. Then a gust of cold wind came under the blinds and caught the paper, tumbling it across the floor. With a cry, the poet scrambled after it, overturning a basket of talismans as she went.

Spring

The tide rises, the tide falls.
This is the spring sea:
Days of tides turning.
                    —*Buson*

NEW YEAR'S DAY

IT WAS DAWN ON THE First Day of the First Month of the New Year. The early rays of sunlight slipped between the palace buildings, their pale pink glow touching the frost on tree branches as if presaging the plum and cherry blossoms to come.

The Emperor sat in the Eastern Garden of the Seriyō Den and looked up at the stars that had not yet been chased away by the morning sun. Among them he found his guardian star. With a pang of sweet memory, he recalled the night, so long ago, that he learned of it. His father had taken him on his lap and pointed to the sky, saying, "See that point of light, my son—the bright one there, by The Weaver. That is your guardian star." And his father had whispered the star's secret name to him, and said, "May it guide you to wisdom, now and when you become Emperor in my place." The Emperor idly wondered if the star had guided to him the little flute player who had made him happy again.

The Emperor faced south, toward the great Shrine of Ise, and softly intoned the secret name of his star. Then he bowed twice in each of the four cardinal directions, once to the heavens and once to the earth. He bowed to the burial place of his ancestors, saying, "Revered Ones, may this year of my reign bring greater prosperity to our empire, which you have given me as my heritage. And may no evil spirits or demons find their way into our land, to disturb the peace of our palace, our capital, or our empire."

Sitting up, the Emperor gazed once more into the morning sky, and saw a bright shooting star fall from near The Weaver towards the northeast.

An omen! thought the Emperor. *The Weaver is of yin nature, and the northeast is an unlucky direction. Yet the star moves from the realm of Tsuki-yomi, Kami of Darkness, towards the realm of Amaterasu, Kami of the Sun and Grandmother of all Emperors. What can this mean?*

Picking up a bundle beside him, the Emperor rose and walked across the garden to the Imperial Shrine. Passing beneath the torii, the sakaki trees, and the carved gates, the Emperor prepared his mind to commune with his sacred Ancestress. He paused at the ablution pavillion to ritually cleanse his hands and mouth. Then, removing his shoes, eboshi cap and court cloak, he entered the shrine.

Waiting to meet him was Nakatomi, High Priest of the Imperial Shrine. Nakatomi was an elderly man, and had inherited his position. *But not without some help from the Fujiwara,* the Emperor thought sardonically.

The Emperor followed the old priest into the sanctuary. He kneeled on a cushion and removed from the bundle he carried a bolt of damask silk of the purest white. The priest took this and approached the altar. On the altar there stood a cabinet of gold and cedarwood. Within the cabinet lay the Octagonal Mirror, the sacred shintai of Amaterasu.

The Emperor wished that the cabinet would be opened, so that he might see again the beautiful golden face of the Sun Kami. But the cabinet was only opened at times of great national import, and he had only seen the Mirror once, on the day that he had become Emperor.

As the priest placed the silk cloth on the altar, the Emperor thought he could see glimmers of pale golden sunlight through the seams of the cabinet.

"Amaterasu is pleased with your offering," the priest said. Together he and the Emperor said prayers for the New Year. Then the priest said, "Do you have anything you wish to ask?"

"Yes. This morning I received what I believe to be an omen," and the Emperor described the shooting star. "Does this have meaning?"

The priest bowed and turned back to the altar. The Emperor thought he saw the priest's cheeks twitch as he chanted, but in the gloom of the shrine he could not be sure. After a minute the priest faced the Emperor again and said, "The meaning is this: Soon you will again have an empress and she will bear you a son, who will be emperor after you."

And who told you to give me this meaning, Amaterasu or Daimigi-san? "Is that all? I detected ill aspects in the omen."

"There are . . . elements of conflict, Your Majesty, but that is the basic meaning."

Naturally there will be conflict. I do not want Daimigi's daughter.

"Is there anything else you would ask, Your Majesty?"

What I truly wish to ask I dare not say in front of you. "No, but I shall offer a private prayer before I go." Bowing deeply, the Emperor thought, *Amaterasu, Mother of the Sun and Holy Grandmother to all emperors, if there is mercy within you I pray that you free this humble descendant from the smothering yoke of the Fujiwara and restore to me the power that is the birthright of your children.* Then the Emperor rose and returned to the Seriyō Den.

Laid out on a low table in the Private Dining Chamber were dishes of rice cakes, radishes and melons, all considered auspicious for ensuring good health during the year. A cluster of cups held various types of spiced wine prepared by the Palace Medicinal Office. Sipping from a cup, the Emperor wondered if it were true that the wine had been tasted by specially chosen virgins before being given to him. The wine was said to be an elixir of long life. *It would be useful if that were more than fable,* thought the Emperor. Today began his forty-first year of life—long past the age at which the last few emperors had abdicated (at the behest of the Fujiwara) to pursue their own interests. *I might have done so, too, had I a son.* Thirty years of married life had produced several daughters but only a few sickly, short-lived sons. *I suppose I should not be surprised that Daimigi is putting on the pressure.*

His Majesty had now and then entertained flights of fancy in which, flying in the face of Buddhist doctrine, he made his eldest daughter Empress Regent. There had been worthy empresses in the past—such as the mighty

Empress Jingo who had led her army on military expeditions to Korea five hundred years before. *But no, the Fujiwara would never accept such a thing, and my daughter would be driven into abdication and exile. It could even bring the warrior-priests snarling down from Mount Hiei to "cleanse" the city of its "evil influences."*

A little page boy in a bright red robe and shoulder-length hair appeared by the sliding door. "His Lordship Fujiwara no Daimigi-sama and his sons have arrived, Your Imperial Majesty, to pay their respects for the New Year. They await audience with you."

No doubt he has by now discovered my little changes in the promotions proceedings for tomorrow. Well, Daimigi-san, I shall have to keep you waiting a day longer before you have an explanation from me. The Emperor turned to the page and said, "Tell Daimigi-san that I have been given an omen of great import. I will be observing a day of abstinence to meditate on its meaning. Please extend my regrets that I may not receive today the respects of him and his sons."

And his sons, echoed the Emperor enviously in his mind as the page left to deliver his message. *Kazenatsu, Hidoi and Korimizu—all healthy lads. What karma gave Daimigi such sons?* Setting down his wine cup, the Emperor retired to his private chambers.

Imperial Promotions

Daimigi's mood was as black as his robes and as chill as the frosty morning dampness that clung to them. Sourly he watched the Great Hall of the Palace of Administration fill with expectant nobles, their blue, yellow-green or black robes flitting colorfully between the huge red lacquer pillars. The eager bobbing of their eboshi hats reminded him of a farmyard of black-combed roosters. *They are warmed by the fires of hope, no doubt.*

The cold of the stone floor seeped up through the straw mat on which Daimigi sat. The small brazier before him gave him no warmth or comfort, nor did the close presence of his three sons beside him. He was all too aware of the curious stares of the other nobles as they noticed he was not seated on the dais of state, where he normally should be on this day.

Impatiently tapping his thigh with his ivory baton of office, Daimigi looked at the great dais at the head of the hall. *Yes. There is where I should be seated, not out here with the rest of this rabble.* It was the duty of the Minister of the Right, along with the Ministers of the Center and the Left, to hand out the important promotions for the year. But now the low platform, Daimigi noticed, had been furnished with the porcelain statues of the Korean Lion and the Fu Dog that always adorned an imperial dais. At the back of the platform stood a golden, many-paneled screen, on which hung the Sacred Imperial Sword.

So. You have been clever, Your Majesty. While I was fruitlessly chasing flautists, you secretly altered the list of preparations and made it appear to be my orders. The reason given for the change is that I had supposedly learned that I, myself would receive promotion. Naturally, it would be unseemly for me to promote myself, and I must receive the office from a superior. Therefore it was only logical that this year's promotions should flow from the Imperial hand.

Across the hall, the Ministers of the Center and the Left, a Minamoto and an Oe, were eyeing Daimigi suspiciously. *They believe I have denied them their duty for selfish reasons. Were I to tell them the truth, they would think me weak, unable to control an upstart emperor. Either way I lose their favor. Very clever, Your Majesty . . . but you forget I have played this game far longer than you.*

At that moment a gong sounded and ten of the Emperor's ladies-in-waiting, dressed in many layers of red and white kimonos, bustled into the hall. Two of them carried cushions and one carried a large, gold lacquer box. The rest carried bundles and parcels and baskets that were clearly gifts for the courtiers. There came scattered cries of "How generous is His Majesty!" and "How fortunate we are to live during the reign of such a noble liege!"

Daimigi scowled. The Day of Promotions was meant to be a dignified occasion, not a festival. He noticed the ladies-in-waiting place two cushions at the front of the dais, then they decorously seated themselves behind the golden screen. *Interesting,* thought the Minister, *Will His Majesty seek to make amends by allowing me to join him on the dais after I am promoted?*

Another gong sounded and the Emperor himself entered. Immediately all bowed deeply, foreheads touching the floormats. Even from this position, Daimigi watched the Emperor warily.

His Majesty was wearing a magnificent court cloak of deep purple silk brocade and under-robes of gold and white. The bottom of his wide left sleeve bulged heavily, and Daimigi assumed there were more gifts hidden there. But, to the Minister's shock, as the Emperor sat and opened his sleeve, the cat Hinata jumped out and sat herself with all feline dignity upon the other cushion. A few chuckles were heard at the back of the hall, but the Emperor silenced them with one dark look.

What does he mean by this? thought Daimigi. *Does he think to insult the Fujiwara by preferring a cat to sit at his side?*

The Emperor rapped the edge of the dais twice with

his fan and all the assembled nobles looked up. A young, blue-robed clerk from the Household Office came to the foot of the dais and opened the gold lacquer box. The Emperor reached in and pulled out an ivory baton on which was inscribed the office to be assigned. In a sonorous voice, the Emperor intoned, "Fujiwara no Daimigi!"

The Minister of the Right came forward on his knees to the dais and bowed.

Handing the baton to Daimigi, the Emperor said, "Fujiwara no Daimigi-san, in recognition of your tremendous efforts on behalf of our empire, I have chosen to reinstate the office of Chancellor, which will now be yours."

Daimigi accepted the baton. *Of course. Chancellor is the only position that must be given by the Emperor. Not that this promotion changes anything. It merely formalizes what is already the case.* Daimigi stood and bowed again, then did his Dance of Gratitude, each movement of his arms, each flourish of his fan utterly correct.

As he finished, the Fujiwara looked up, expecting the Emperor to summon him onto the platform to sit beside him for the rest of the proceedings. But the Emperor only nodded solemnly. Daimigi looked pointedly at the cat, who blinked down at him as if wondering whether he would make an amusing toy. The Emperor gave a little cough of impatience, and Daimigi allowed just the slightest shadow of a scowl to cross his face before walking, very slowly, back to his mat.

The new Chancellor had barely reseated himself when the Emperor called out the next name.

"Fujiwara no Kazenatsu!"

As the handsome eldest son went forward and bowed, the Emperor held out a baton and said, "As your father is vacating the post of Minister of the Right, this office shall be yours."

Daimigi gave a small sigh of relief. At least this promotion had been expected. *Perhaps the presence of the cat is only a childish act of defiance. Very well, Your Majesty. You may play your little game . . . but do not expect to win.*

Daimigi watched Kazenatsu do his Dance of Gratitude. *So graceful and elegant you are! What a fine young emperor you would make. If we could but marry you to His Majesty's eldest daughter, and then force him to abdicate . . . but no. The other great families would never stand for so obvious a ploy, and they would be down on our necks instantly. No, for the safety of our family and the purity of the imperial line things must be done this way, and I must rest content with my grandson-to-be as emperor.*

Kazenatsu returned to his place and the Emperor called the next name. "Echizen no Netsubo!"

The Minister of the Imperial Grounds came forward—almost too eagerly, Daimigi noted—and bowed. "As the office of Minister of the Imperial Household has been left vacant due to retirement, that office is now yours, and you are now Fourth Rank." The Emperor handed Netsubo the ivory baton, and a clerk rushed forward bearing the black Senior Courtier's over-robe. This was draped over Netsubo's shoulders as he began his Dance of Gratitude.

Daimigi observed that Netsubo's dance was correct, but just a bit obsequious. *This one clearly hungers for position. One wonders if his flute-playing daughter is merely a ploy to make him noticed at court. It seems to have succeeded.*

When Netsubo finished, the Emperor gestured with his fan for him to wait. "Netsubo-san, before you go, I would like to ask you a question. Why did you not tell us you had such a talented daughter?"

Netsubo flushed and bowed to hide it. "Your Majesty,

I . . . I wanted to be certain she was of sufficient skill before presenting her to the Court."

Various snorts and mutterings of disbelief erupted in the back of the hall. The Emperor rapped the edge of the dais with his fan for silence and said, "Well, if my own humble opinion is of any value, I would say she is skilled enough. And I am eager to have her installed at Court as soon as we may."

Netsubo gave a proud smile and bowed deeply. "Your kind words honor this one's family, Your Majesty."

Hidoi murmured, "It will be nice having Uguisu at Court, though if His Majesty wants her I suppose I won't have much chance—"

"Hush, my son," Daimigi hissed, "His Majesty no doubt merely wishes her services as a musician." Irritated that he had missed what the Emperor had said next, Daimigi frowned at Hidoi and leaned forward to listen.

"Of course," the Emperor was saying, idly examining his fan, "if your daughter pleases me, there is no need for her to retain the lowly status of Imperial Lady."

Daimigi nearly fell over with shock, and there were gasps around the hall. The only rank above imperial lady was empress! *He wouldn't dare! Does he think to ruin us all? Does he truly think the Court would accept a girl of an unimportant family as empress, or any son of hers as emperor?*

Netsubo bowed his way back to his seat. The Emperor called upon Minamotos, Tairas, Oes, and other nobles of great families, as Daimigi seethed and worried.

What can he hope to accomplish? If he does not take my daughter, and the court does not accept Uguisu, and he dies without an acceptable heir, what then? The nearest relative is a nephew out in the provinces who is the son of the Emperor's younger sister and a Minamoto! Daimigi shut his eyes and sighed. So far, the warlike Minamoto had been content with their position as "the teeth and claws of the Fujiwara." But to give them such a foothold on the throne would be disastrous.

Daimigi's mind wandered further along these paths until his attention snapped back as Hidoi's name was called. Hidoi nearly leapt to his feet and scampered up to the Emperor, sliding into his bow.

Too eager, my son. You must never look too eager. When will you learn this?

The Emperor took a baton of polished wood out of the lacquered box, then paused. "Hidoi-san, you are currently the Junior Assistant Minister of Central Affairs, are you not?"

Hidoi looked up from his deep bow, confused. "Yes, Your Majesty."

"Ah. Well, then, the court is pleased to inform you that you are *still* Junior Assistant Minister of Central Affairs."

Hidoi seemed frozen in mid-bow as he heard this, except for his eyes that darted back and forth, as if hoping someone would come forward to tell him what to do. "Your Majesty?"

Daimigi resisted the urge to glare openly at the Emperor. For a Fujiwara not to be promoted as a matter of course every year was practically an insult, or evidence of royal disfavor. *Has Hidoi's offensiveness become too much? Or is this arrow aimed, instead, at me?*

Hidoi slowly rose and did a too-brief, awkward Dance of Gratitude before slinking back to his father's side. "What have I done?" he whispered to Daimigi. "Is he doing this just so he won't have to compete with me over Uguisu?"

"Don't flatter yourself, boy. We will sort this out later. Just be grateful you were not made a provincial governor."

"But, father, I was supposed to become Minister of Imperial Grounds now that—"

"Hush, I say!" The fact that the Emperor was staring at them with a wry twist to his mouth did not improve Daimigi's humor. He waited through more names from other families until his youngest son was called. Fifteen-year-old Korimizu received the title of Chief of Imperial Guard. Daimigi pondered this as Korimizu did his Dance of Gratitude with solemn dignity and considerable grace for his age. *He will be a fine figure in time. The post is an honorable one for a boy his age, no matter what is thought of the Ministry of War.* Feeling there was no further reason to remain, Daimigi and his sons rose to leave.

Just then, the Emperor called out, "Niwa-san!"

Silence fell on the hall and no one moved as the wiry old man entered and came before the Imperial dais. *Is he insane? A commoner in the Promotions?* thought the Fujiwara.

"Niwa-san, because of your great assistance to the Court in discovering Uguisu, I would honor you by promoting you to the office of Minister of Imperial Grounds."

Daimigi sucked in his breath. *So that is why he wished to deny Hidoi that title.*

"Gracious Majesty," said the old gardener. "Niwa is undeserving of this honor."

I could not agree more, thought Daimigi.

"Nonsense," said the Emperor. "You have served me and my Court faithfully for as long as I can remember. I would say you are long overdue for this. And it is time a man of your venerable age be allowed a more dignified life than filling the demands for poem blossoms from us younger folk."

"It has always pleased Niwa to serve the Gentlemen Who Dwell Among the Clouds in whatever way Niwa may."

"And now we may return the favor. What of your son Takenoko? Where is he? I would honor him also."

"Glorious Majesty, he has honored this family enough by leaving this world to become a monk at the Temple of Ninna-ji." Niwa did not even attempt a Dance of Gratitude, but only bowed himself out of the hall, his new green cloak of office draped over his shoulders.

Well, he is old, thought Daimigi, *and cannot be expected to remain in office long. I can take some consolation in that.*

Just then, four ladies-in-waiting brought in a large, four-paneled kicho, within which a woman hesitantly walked. "I realize," the Emperor said, "that ladies generally receive their promotions on the eighth of this month. However there is one special exception I wished to make. Katte-san!"

Daimigi clenched his fists at his sides. *A woman! A commoner woman at the Imperial Promotions! He is mad, for certain.* Then Daimigi felt his heart grow cool and he almost smiled. *Of course. Your Majesty has gone the step too far. You have given me the very weapons with which I will win your game. Others will see the folly of giving political decisions to an emperor. And when I take steps to "correct" your errors, none will hinder me.*

Hidoi craned his neck, bobbing his head around, trying to get a glance of the woman within. Daimigi soundly thwacked Hidoi on the shoulder with his fan. "You are in the Imperial Presence, boy! You are Fujiwara! Act with the dignity required!"

Hidoi winced and cowered. Kazenatsu, however, was only slightly more restrained in his curiosity, as were most of the nobles in the room.

"Katte-san!" the Emperor called again, and one of the ladies-in-waiting nudged and whispered to the woman inside the kicho. A tremulous, soft voice said, "The lowly one you speak of is here, Most Glorious Majesty."

"Well, 'that lowly one' shall be lowly no more. In honor of your help in finding the flute player Uguisu when no one else could, I appoint you Mistress of the Imperial Kitchens. You are now Myobu no Katte, and a lady of the Fifth Rank."

Gasps and exclamations swept the hall. Some nobles nodded with appreciation, while others frowned in disapproval. *It's that daughter of Netsubo's,* thought Daimigi, coldly. *His Majesty is so infatuated with her that he no longer thinks of propriety or duty. She is another knot that we must see undone.*

"I should also like to mention at this time," the Emperor said, "that my eldest daughter is to become High Priestess of the great Kamo Shrine."

Daimigi decided he did not need to hear any more. With every indication of wounded dignity, he stood. Making a cursory bow to the Emperor, Daimigi swept out of the hall, plans already filling his mind.

Further Instructions

Uguisu started at every creak of wood, every sigh of wind through the eaves, as she crept through the abandoned house. The sweet scent of plum blossoms from the wild garden outside made Uguisu imagine that ghosts of perfumed ladies wandered the empty corridors with her. She wondered if more spirits would be in attendance this night than the one she intended to summon.

Uguisu made her way through a maze of broken shoji to the center of the house, where she was less likely to be observed, by the mortal world at least. The wood floor was bare and splintered, and the walls bore the slashmarks of intruding thieves. Uguisu brought out from under her kimono the heavy mirror she carried and leaned it against a wall.

During the Festival of U-Bon it had been safe to use a fire in the garden. But this night, even in this deserted part of town, a fire would be noticed. The mirror would be just as useful, for mirrors were by nature somewhat magical. But Uguisu felt a subtle fear that the mirror would be more than just a window to the Underworld.

Quickly she laid out the seven herbs and incense sticks before the mirror, then sat back on her heels to wait. Moonlight streamed in through cracks in the roof, making Uguisu's reflection appear pale and ghostly in the mirror.

After many long moments, Uguisu felt a prickling up her back and saw in the mirror a cloudy shape forming over her right shoulder. She had an intense urge to turn and look behind her but did not, for she knew it would break the spell. The cloudy form shifted and resolved into the craggy face and hands of her guardian spirit.

"Greetings, Uguisu." The voice was a reedy whisper on the wind.

"Blessing upon you, Wise One." Uguisu bowed to the mirror.

"Ah, it is too late for that, little one."

Odd gusts of wind rustled Uguisu's voluminous robes, and she asked, "Are there other spirits in this house, Wise One?"

The face in the mirror gave a little smile. "There are kami everywhere, Uguisu, as all things have kami. But surely you did not summon me to discuss religion?"

"No, Wise One. My father has told me that I am at last invited to Court. I am to become an Imperial Lady . . . and may become Empress! It has all happened as you said. I was found and I played the flute for them, and now the Emperor wants me at Court. You said that I should speak to you again when this was accomplished."

"Hai, Uguisu. You have done very well. Now you shall learn of the purpose for which you have been so carefully prepared.

"You will indeed become Empress, and you will bear the Emperor a son who will be the Crown Prince."

Uguisu gasped. Bowing very low, she said, "I am deeply honored, Wise One."

"Yes, you are. But not for the reasons you think.

"Seven generations ago, during the reign of Emperor Shomu, the Fujiwara were striving to gain the power they now possess. However, there was one among the Imperial family who opposed them. His name was Prince Nagaya, and he was a skillful student of sorcery. The Fujiwara feared him, for he was the only one who might thwart their ambitions. One night, while Prince Nagaya was absorbed in his magical studies, Fujiwara no Umaki took the troops of the Six Headquarters of the Guards and surrounded the prince's house. After extensive interrogation by three nobles, Prince Nagaya was forced to confess that he planned to use his sorcery to overthrow the State. He was condemned to death by strangulation. Shortly thereafter, a law was passed saying that those caught 'practising mysterious arts' would be severely punished."

"But what has this to do with me."

"Prince Nagaya was my son, Uguisu, and your distant ancestor. Yes, little one, your mother's family is of royal blood."

Uguisu's eyes opened wide, first with surprise, then anger. "Why wasn't I told this before? Didn't my father know? Why have we suffered from the obscurity of my mother's family, when it would have helped my father's ambitions and I could have served at Court much sooner?"

"Patience, child! You rant from ignorance, and there is more to tell. Because sorcery was our family's area of learning, we were banished from the capital and sent to a faraway province. We were forbidden to return, or else the entire family would be put to the sword. So, far in the mountains we stayed, honing our sorcerous skills while concealing our identity. And we taught our daughters poetry, music and other gentle arts to give them prospects of noble marriage. In this way, we hoped to return to Heian Kyo, for vengeance still burned in our hearts. Though my body long ago passed into ashes, my soul has chosen to remain tied to this world, to guide Nagaya's daughters toward our goal."

"Vengeance?" Uguisu asked, hoping she had misunderstood.

The ghost ignored her and continued. "Our progress was difficult and we met with no success, our clan dwindling until only your mother was left. Then your father, Netsubo, became governor of our province. Your mother had no trouble beguiling him into marriage, and when he was called back to the capital, we had the highest hopes. Alas, your mother did not take the journey well, and she died before much could be accomplished."

"I remember," Uguisu murmured, seeing in her mind her beautiful mother dying in the elegant ox-cart meant for their triumphal entry into the capital.

"But your mother did give us you. And she provided for you even as she parted from this world. Her death curse was that your father would be filled with ambition. In this way, you would still have noble prospects of marriage, and your father would be too busy to burden you with an unkind stepmother. And so it has come to pass."

Uguisu was silent a moment as she absorbed what had been said. "So, when I become Empress, my mother's

family can be known and returned to its rightful place of
nobility. In this way, Prince Nagaya shall be avenged
against the Fujiwara who thought they had destroyed us.
Is this what you are saying?"

The spirit erupted into a hissing, cackling laughter that
made Uguisu jump in fear. "Ah, the simple minds of
children. An elegant revenge that would be indeed, were
position enough to forgive all. The Fujiwara have not
forgotten Prince Nagaya. What makes you think that
being Empress will save you from the executioner's sword,
once your mother's family is identified? By returning our
family to the Nine-Fold Enclosure, you will become a
criminal, Uguisu."

Uguisu felt her mouth drop open. "But . . . but—"

"Fear not. I did not guide you all this way to suffer
meaningless humiliation and death. Did I not say you
would bear the Emperor a son? Well, this shall be no
ordinary infant. The babe will not have a spirit of its own.
When it is conceived the child will be possessed by the
spirit of Prince Nagaya himself. It is he, my own son, who
shall issue forth from you and become the next Emperor,
though his way be paved with the blood of the Fujiwara,
and the puppet Emperor they now support. *This* will be
our revenge, Uguisu—the destruction of the Fujiwara
family, as they would have destroyed us, and the gaining
of the imperial throne for Prince Nagaya, just as they had
feared seven generations ago. He and I will be satisfied
with nothing less."

"But . . . I . . . I cannot kill—"

"That is not your task, Uguisu. You are the fire in
which our sword of vengeance will be forged. Though
Nagaya will have the body of a babe, yet he will retain the
knowledge of his past life. And he shall also have the

sorcerous skills he has learned during his sojourn in the Underworld. It is he who will do these things."

Uguisu saw in her mind the Emperor's face, the beautiful tear on his cheek. "But . . . must His Majesty . . ."

"It is true he is no friend of the Fujiwara. But he would not stand for a demon-child inheriting his throne in place of a real son of his own. He would interfere. No, Uguisu. The Emperor must die."

Ceremony of the Blue Horses

Plum blossoms shone magenta against the bright blue spring morning sky. As if to dim their early glory, artificial cherry blossoms of pale pink and white were draped along the eaves of the palace buildings, along the main route into the Nine-Fold Enclosure. The full contingent of palace guards lined this route, their lacquered armor glistening in the sunlight. Lieutenant Kuma stood among them, breathing the crisp morning air, pleased to be a part of his favorite festival of the year.

Beneath the paper cherry blossoms, on the veranda of the Seriyō Den, sat the assembled palace nobility—chamberlains, ministers, the highest of the Gentlemen Who Dwell Among The Clouds. And in their center sat the Emperor himself, smiling and passing a small bottle of sake. *There will be much of that flowing today*, thought Kuma with an anticipatory smile.

Behind and to either side of the group of seated gentlemen were gaily painted bamboo blinds, beneath which could be seen the trailing edges of elegant kimono sleeves, indicating where the ladies were seated. Kuma wondered if any of those colorful garments belonged to his Katte, so newly made a Lady.

Somewhere a gong sounded and there came the sound

of clopping hooves and nervous snorts from down the broad pathway. A cheer rose from the guards and noblemen as a parade of twenty-one horses was brought down the pathway, led by the stablemasters in stiff ceremonial costume. Sunlight flickered off the steel blue coats of the horses. Some of the guardsmen twanged their bowstrings to make the horses prance and toss their manes.

From the veranda, the Emperor shouted words of encouragement, wishing the stablemen, guards and assembled nobility long life and good health through the coming year. The guardsmen cheered and chanted the Emperor's name.

Kuma joined in the shouting throng, thinking about the archery competitions and horse races to come later that day. Suddenly he felt a tugging at his elbow. Looking behind him, he saw a blue-robed clerk with a worried expression.

"Lieutenant Kuma-san, you are wanted in the Captain General's office immediately."

Kuma felt his stomach knot. *The Captain General is that young son of the Chancellor . . . the one who saw me in the Fujiwara Palace!* Kuma had hoped to avoid encountering the new Captain General since Korimizu's promotion. Now he had no choice. *Today of all days.* With a regretful glance back at the horses, Kuma trudged to the Palace of Administration.

Kuma stepped briskly into the building and let himself be guided by a page boy down a dark wooden corridor. He presently came to a spacious room, half of which was lined with cabinets and drawers stuffed to overflowing with papers.

On the other side of the room was a low dais, on which sat the new Captain General and beside him the new Household Minister Netsubo. The Fujiwara boy seemed nearly lost in his voluminous green robes of office, and the eboshi cap sat too far back on his head.

Kuma entered and bowed, wishing he could hide his face. "You sent for me, My Lord General?"

The boy looked up and raised his eyebrows in surprise. "You are Lieutenant Kuma of the Inner Guard?" His voice was a pleasant tenor.

Hm. I am recognized, yet unexpected. Perhaps it is not as I fear. "Yes, my lord."

"I have called you before me on a serious matter that has come to my attention."

"My Lord?" Kuma had to admit it was a tribute to Fujiwara training that the boy managed to carry himself with dignity.

Korimizu looked at Netsubo. "You are certain this is the one?"

The Household Minister nodded. "Hai, Korimizu-san. That one."

The boy-general looked back at Kuma and continued, "It has come to our attention that you knew the current Mistress of Imperial Kitchens, the Lady Katte, before she brought Netsubo's daughter Uguisu to the attention of the court."

Now what is the significance of this? Sudden suspicion shot through Kuma's heart. *Do the Fujiwara seek to punish me by humiliating Katte? Do the court snobs find her common past so unacceptable that they now wish to harass her with scandal? Well they shall get no help from me!* "I was aware of her existence, yes."

Netsubo blatantly stifled a snort.

The boy frowned. "We have heard, Kuma-san, that your knowledge of the lady was somewhat more . . . intimate."

Kuma wondered nastily if the boy knew what the word

meant. "What makes the acquaintances of my past a 'serious matter,' My Lord?"

Korimizu looked at Netsubo again, who gestured for him to continue. "When Netsubo was conducting his search for the flute player, you were asked to assist, were you not?"

Now what has that to do with anything? "Yes, My Lord."

"Lord Netsubo himself asked you to search for someone who had heard of the flute player, did he not?"

"Yes, My Lord."

"Yet, all this time, you were 'acquainted' with the one person who did know the whereabouts and identity of the flute player. But you did not tell Lord Netsubo about her, did you?"

"But My Lord—"

"Did you?"

"My Lord, I could not—"

"Did you?"

Kuma sighed heavily. "No, My Lord." He glared at Netsubo. *And am I to take the blame because you did not know it was your own daughter?*

The boy nodded in grave satisfaction, as if he had finally heard the answer he expected.

Kuma quickly added, "Katte-san never told me about the flute player. I had no way of knowing she knew."

"You expect us to believe this, when you have been . . . intimate with her?"

Kuma decided the boy definitely did not know what the word meant. "It is truth, my lord. *Honto des'*."

"Hmm." Korimizu took a scroll from Netsubo's hand. "I have here a decree from Chancellor Daimigi, urging all departments to rid themselves of untrustworthy elements. Because we find your testimony suspect, you are no longer Guards Lieutenant Kuma. You are now simply

Guardsman Kuma. And if any more suspicion falls on you, you will no longer be even that. This meeting is at an end. Return to your duties."

Kuma bowed, his face hot with anger and humiliation. He tried to think of a scathing reply, but knew such words would only bring further punishment.

"Go now."

In one swift motion, Kuma rose and rushed from the room, storming out of the Palace of Administration. *It could have been worse,* he tried to convince himself. *But fortunately the Fujiwara themselves could not admit that they had been tricked. Their revenge must be subtle. But why in the name of all the aspects of holy Buddha did they have to drag Katte into it?*

Too angry to think clearly, Kuma did not return to his post. Instead, his feet led him towards the one who could ease his mind.

As he strode into the women's quarters, two ladies-in-waiting valiantly tried to block his way.

"Really, sir, you cannot just come barging in like this!"

"This is most irregular! Please, consider your actions, sir!"

"I want to see the Lady Katte-san. At once!"

"Myobu Katte-san is not prepared to receive visitors, sir."

"Really," put in the other lady, "do you think she is some common criminal or prisoner that you can make demands of her?"

Barely controlling his anger, Kuma said, "Tell her it is Kuma-san who has come to see her. She will speak to me!"

The ladies began to protest further when Katte's voice came from a room down the corridor. "What is happening? Kuma-san?"

"One moment," the ladies said to Kuma, and they hurried down the corridor, whispering loudly to one another. "Really, and in broad daylight!"

"I suppose it is what comes of making a commoner a lady."

"Well, I hope we do not have to suffer much of this. There will be too much talk."

They had disappeared behind a shoji. Kuma crossed his arms and leaned back against a cypress pillar, listening to their muffled voices and the sounds of shifting furniture.

After a minute, the ladies-in-waiting returned and beckoned to him. Kuma was led into a dark, well-furnished room, containing a large, teak wardrobe, a low table, lacquered boxes of many drawers, and a beautiful, silk-paneled kicho. Kuma was led to a cushion before the screen. He sat, noting an elegant perfume wafting from behind the silk panels. Kuma imagined what Katte must look like in fine robes and was certain she would be beautiful indeed. "Katte-san?"

"Kuma-chan," her voice was soft, and a little frightened. "You should not have come here like this. There will be gossip."

"There is always gossip," Kuma said. He looked at the kicho with irritation. "Do we need this screen, Katte-san? It is not as if I am a stranger to you. Can I not see you? We have been face to face before—"

The ladies-in-waiting, kneeling at either side of the kicho, sucked in their breaths and clicked their tongues. Kuma glared at them.

"You must not speak like this, Kuma-san," said Katte. "I am a Myobu, now. A Lady of the Fifth Rank must behave with dignity. We cannot be as . . . familiar as before."

Kuma supressed an urge to fling the kicho aside. Now

that he was near Katte, he could not think of what to say. He knew he should warn her. But he could not bring himself to discuss his humiliation. Instead, he said, "Your rise in position is good fortune for us, Katte-san. My family will no longer have any objections to our marriage, if you are willing."

More disapproving noises came from the ladies, and Katte said, "You should not speak so boldly, Kuma-san. Though I may be willing, my family will now have objections. Now that I am in the palace, they hope I will catch a bigger fish. They have heard that the Household Minister, Netsubo, has been a widower a long time. They say it is unnatural that a man should be so long without a wife."

"Netsubo?" Kuma growled, gripping his knees tightly. *Is this why he was overseer at my demotion?*

"I do not know if I can deny my family's wishes, Kuma-san. I do not know . . . what will happen."

Kuma felt at a loss for words. Taking paper, brush and inkstone from the low table, he wrote:

"My caterpillar has become a butterfly. See!
How beautiful her wings,
with which she flies beyond my reach."

Kuma slipped the paper beneath a panel of the kicho, and silently rose to leave. As he reached the doorway, he heard the ladies discussing his poem's lack of literary merit, and quiet sobbing from behind the silk kicho.

Uguisu Comes To Court

The ceremonial procession was magnificent indeed as it slowly made its way down the broad Suzaku Oji toward the Imperial Palace. Nearly a hundred outriders in elaborate court costume rode at the head of the parade. Behind them came carriages of silk, palm leaves, and split bamboo—some were gilded and some had carved wooden eaves. The oxen that drew them wore garlands of plum and cherry blossoms, and the ox-drivers wore their finest homespuns. To those who watched, it seemed even the willow trees that lined the great avenue bowed in honor of the opulence passing by them.

But to Uguisu, seated within a curtained carriage at the center of the procession, the lavish display brought only shame. *I am a mother tiger, being brought into a forest of deer where my cub shall feast upon their blood.* She felt lost in the twelve layers of unlined silk robes she wore. Her cheeks felt clammy from the white face powder. Her scalp itched where her hair was bound with golden combs and pins. Netsubo had spared no expense for Uguisu's ceremony, and she wondered if he resented the outlay of so much wealth. She almost wished he hadn't bothered.

"You should let your sleeves drape outside the curtains," said her maid Tetsuda, who sat across from her in the carriage. "That way others can imagine and admire your beauty."

Uguisu allowed the maid to slip the edges of her sleeves beneath the curtains. She found it ironic that now that she was made up as a magnificent lady, it was all the more important that no man see her. All that could be safely displayed were her sleeves.

Uguisu heard a bump-bump from the carriages ahead and her heart went cold. They were crossing the ground beam of the Taiken Mon, the Central Gate into the Greater Imperial Palace. As her own cart jolted through the gate, Uguisu felt she had crossed a bridge into a new, terrifying period in her life—a bridge she could never recross.

Presently her carriage was pulled alongside one wing of

one of the palaces—she had no idea which—and she was helped out by several ladies-in-waiting. For only a few seconds she was exposed to view, and then she was led down a dim corridor to a large, central chamber. There Uguisu was installed behind a magnificent kicho whose frame was carved cypress and whose panels were deep purple silk, embroidered with gold and scarlet thread. Yet it did not please Uguisu, and she found herself missing her plain, faded kicho at home.

Dishes of rice, fish and vegetables were brought to her. But despite her hunger, Uguisu could only take small samples of each, for ladies were not supposed to enjoy eating.

For interminable hours Uguisu sat, as visitors approached her screen. Monks came and chanted sutras of blessing. Noblemen whom Uguisu had never heard of came and left lavish gifts of silver and silk, perhaps hoping she would speak well of them to the Emperor. Uguisu felt distant from it all, as if it were happening to someone else. *Surely I, daughter of witches, do not deserve any of this.*

When the Emperor himself came by to pay his respects, Uguisu froze in fear. But all he said was, "We look forward to your song this evening, little nightingale," and he was gone. Uguisu felt guilt settle heavily on her heart, for she wished she could again see his face. Yet she knew it was best that she did not.

After all the other presentations, Netsubo came behind her screen, as was his right as father. Facing her, he handed to Uguisu the ceremonial white silk trousers in honor of her acceptance at court. As Uguisu leaned forward to accept the garment, her father said softly, "I have had doubts about your behavior these past few weeks, Uguisu. But it appears a wise kami is guiding your fate. I am very proud of you, my daughter."

Uguisu bowed deeply to hide her gasp and the brimming of tears in her eyes. Her father had never spoken to her that way. *Will you be so proud of me when Prince Nagaya has done his work? Will he require your death as well?*

"Have you nothing to say to me, Uguisu?"

Trying to control her breathing so she would not speak in sobs, she said, "All that I have done, and will do, is for the greater glory of my family."

Netsubo nodded. "You are a good daughter, Uguisu. Your mother in Heaven must look down on you with pride."

As her father departed, Uguisu covered her face with her sleeves, wishing she could die.

That evening, Uguisu played her flute at her honorary banquet, though etiquette required that she be one room away from where the noblemen ate and drank their wine. She could hear the muffled voices of the Emperor over the chatter and laughter of the women around her, and she wished his voice were not so strong and clear.

Uguisu put down her flute to rest and looked at her new ladies-in-waiting, trying to remember their names. *The plump one—her name is Nikao, "two faces." She is pleasant to look at, but I think she smiles too much. She tries too hard to please me. The narrow-faced one, she is pretty too, but she looks like a fox—ah, Kitsune—that's it. I don't think she likes me. And the third, Shonasaki, she's the nicest of them. But she spends so much time staring at nothing, and then scribbling poems, that I doubt she'll be of much use.*

"You play so beautifully, Lady Uguisu!" said Nikao. "And it is so charmingly appropriate that Our Majesty should lodge you in the Plum Pavillion. The plum tree, after all, is the rightful home of the uguisu, neh?"

Uguisu managed a little smile and picked up the flute

to play again. Suddenly, a small page boy slid aside their shoji and came into the room. He handed Kitsune a piece of folded purple paper that had a sprig of plum blossoms attached. "For the Lady Uguisu, from His Majesty," he whispered loudly.

Nikao giggled into her sleeves. Shonasaki looked up with interest. Kitsune balanced the note on one palm as if deciding whether Uguisu should have it. Uguisu, a cold ball forming in her stomach, didn't want to see it.

"Don't keep us waiting!" said Nikao, snatching the note from Kitsune's hand. "Let's see what it says."

Placing the plum branch gently to one side, Nikao opened it and read:

> "The song of the nightingale is so soft and sweet,
> One wonders if her feathered breast is soft to touch
> as well."

"Ooooh, how lovely," said Nikao, "and such an elegant hand. He never wrote poems like this to our old Empress."

"Hush, Nikao!" chided Kitsune. "You should not speak so about her."

"Well, it's true!"

"It is not important to Our Lady here. You must, of course, answer him, Lady Uguisu."

Uguisu sat utterly still. It was what she feared. His Majesty had the right to ask for her embrace this night. But to fulfill the wishes of her guardian spirit, Uguisu had to deny him until a particular day.

"Would you like me to compose a reply for you, My Lady?" asked Shonasaki.

Uguisu shook herself. "No, thank you." She reached for a writing brush, but as she took it her hand trembled so that she put it down immediately.

"Please allow me, my lady." Shonasaki took the brush and in a spirited hand wrote:

> "The feathers of the nightingale
> Tremble at the winds from Heaven.

Our lady is tired, my lord, from all the ceremony. Have pity and let her rest for now."

Uguisu nodded her approval, wondering how Shonasaki knew her mood.

Kitsune haughtily folded the note, and they decided the best poem gift would be some reeds from a sleeping mat. This was given to the page boy, and he scurried out, sliding the shoji shut behind him.

A moment later, there came an odd scratching on the shoji. As Kitsune opened it a crack, a yellow cat with golden eyes slipped in.

"Ah!" said Nikao, "Lady Hinata graces us with a visit."

The cat gave a perfunctory sniff to each of the ladies' hands, then approached Uguisu. Uguisu reached out to pet Hinata, but the cat drew back out of reach.

"Lady Hinata is very particular about who she befriends," said Kitsune. "She must get to know you first."

So Uguisu sat still as Hinata intently sniffed her clothing and hands, as if conducting a thorough examination. When Hinata reached the flute, she sniffed most carefully indeed. When she raised her head at last, her mouth was slightly open, as if she had caught a whiff of something distasteful.

"She probably dislikes the woodstain," said Nikao shrugging.

The cat sat and stared at Uguisu, and Uguisu felt as though those golden eyes were seeing into her soul. *Amida help me, could this creature actually sense my guilt?* Uguisu felt suddenly afraid.

"She must think highly of you, to gaze at you so," said Nikao.

Hinata gave a little sneeze and swiftly turned away, trotting out past the shoji just as the page boy returned.

This time the note was on white paper, with a pine twig attached. Shonasaki took the note and read:

> "The winds from Heaven shall be stilled by the
> > pines,
> So as not to scare the nightingale away."

"Ah," said Shonasaki, "*Matsu* means 'to wait' as well as 'pine tree.' His Majesty will wait until you are ready."

Uguisu closed her eyes and gave a long sigh. Then, picking up her flute, she played once more.

Ladies of Fashion

The cherry blossoms in the Divine Spring Garden, just south of the Imperial Palace, were in full bloom. Their sweet scent filled the air, and their boughs provided a lavish pink and white canopy against the pale blue sky.

"This was a wonderful idea!" said Nikao, setting down the large picnic boxes she carried. She, Kitsune and Shonasaki settled themselves in a mossy hollow, ringed with cherry trees. They all wore pink and white robes to match the flowers, and Shonasaki imagined that to a bird they would resemble enormous cherry blossoms fallen to earth. As she lay back against the moss, it seemed the world ended at the edge of the hollow, and all of existence was the moss, the trees and the sky.

"Are you sure Lady Uguisu won't notice we're gone?" the poet asked dreamily.

"Hmpf," Kitsune replied, "she's observing another day of abstinence. She'll want to see no one but priests to chant sutras for her."

"That's the third abstinence this month," mused Shonasaki. "What lies so heavy on her heart that she feels she must deprive herself so?"

"Why look at it that way?" said Nikao. "Everyone I talk to admires her devotion and piety."

"She should show such devotion to His Majesty," said Kitsune.

"She's just shy. She has said she will give in to him in time, when she is comfortable here. He doesn't seem to mind."

"Her music is so sad," said Shonasaki. "Even the cheerful saibara she plays have an undertone of sorrow."

"Lady Uguisu has a fine sense of *awaré*, the transience of all things. That only shows she has noble sensitivity. Everyone I talk to—"

"Everyone you talk to knows she is the darling of the Emperor and dares not speak against her!" snapped Kitsune.

"You know that is not so! And you should be glad to be waiting on her, for it reflects well on us. We are at the center of fashion now, as we were when we served the Empress."

"But such fashions!" Kitsune protested. "Some ladies no longer blacken their teeth because she does not. And they now wear sticks of wood painted to look like her flute as netsuke on their sleeves. Men go about whistling the tunes she plays. And a mother-to-be I know says she will name her baby 'Uguisu' whether it is a girl or a boy."

Nikao giggled. "Yes, isn't it delightful? And Shonasaki's

poems about her are being read and praised everywhere. And whenever there is a gathering for gossip we are always invited. You cannot say you do not enjoy the attention we are getting, Kitsune."

"Well," Kitsune said, smoothing a fold in her outermost kimono, "it is true that the Chancellor, Daimigi-sama himself, just the other day approached me. He said he would like to speak with me often, for he wants to know everything that Lady Uguisu does. The Fujiwara have taken a great interest in her, it seems. The Chancellor said that if my conversation pleases him, he would not take it amiss if his son Kazenatsu should choose to spend time with me."

"There, you see?" said Nikao. "Lady Uguisu will bring us nothing but good fortune."

Kitsune smiled a thin smile and looked at Shonasaki.

The poet understood and raised an eyebrow. A cherry blossom, blown free by the wind, drifted down and Shonasaki caught it in her hand. "Then we must beware, Nikao. For it is the essence of *awaré* that all things of beauty and joy must fall."

"In that case," said Nikao, popping a rice ball into her mouth, "we should enjoy the good things while we may."

Summer

Storm-wind walks the fields.
Rising from the cowering grass,
Full moon haunts the night.
—Chora

TEMPLE BLOSSOMS

SPRINGTIME LINGERED ON THE hillsides of Yama-shiro. In the vale of Heian Kyo cherry blossoms were making way for the orange blossoms of summer. But on the slopes surrounding the Temple of Ninna-Ji, the cherry trees and azaleas retained their spring glory.

They, too, are reluctant to leave this world, thought Takenoko.

Takenoko ran a hand over his tonsured hair and looked down at his grey robe. *Would anyone from my past recognize me now?*

Sighing, he took up his rake again, and continued drawing fine lines through the white sand of the temple garden. *No matter that I am now a student to a master priest. I am still a gardener.*

He raked up to a large plum tree and noticed that it stubbornly bore some purple blossoms, though it was long past the time they should have fallen. Takenoko plucked one of the flowers and smelled its fading perfume. "The orange blossom is supposed to be the flower of reminiscence," he murmured to the plum flower, "yet you remain to cruelly bring me thoughts of one I left behind."

Just days before, a pilgrim had come to the temple and spoke of rumors that Uguisu had gone to live in the Imperial Palace. *I suppose that means her father made her marry Hidoi.* Takenoko sighed again and whispered, "Uguisu."

There came a gentle cough behind him, and Takenoko jumped. He saw the old priest who had become his teacher standing there, leaning on a wooden staff. He wore an amused smile.

"Er, I was just thinking of the bird that is commonly associated with plum trees," Takenoko blurted. "The uguisu, you know."

"Were you?" said the priest. "Let me tell you an old story."

Takenoko closed his eyes. *Not another story!*

The old priest cleared his throat and began. "Once there was a master and his student, and they were walking along a lonely mountain path. Presently they came to a rushing stream, for it was spring and much water came down from the mountains. On their side of the stream stood a woman in bright kimonos. She said to them, 'Excuse, me, good sirs, but I cannot cross the stream, for it would sweep me away. Could one of you please help me cross?'

"So, the master took her upon his back and the three of them crossed the rushing stream. On the other side, the master set the woman down and he and the student continued on their way.

"But many ri later, the student turned to the master and said angrily, 'How could you do that? I thought we are not supposed to touch women! How could you do such a thing?'

"And the master turned to the student and said, 'I left the woman by the side of the stream. Why do you continue to carry her?' "

The old priest then nodded at Takenoko and walked away across the garden.

Takenoko blinked and breathed, "Why do I still carry her?" Reluctantly, he allowed the plum blossom to fall from his hand and he took up his rake again.

Winding Water Banquet

"She still denies you?" Daimigi said.

"Mmmmm?" replied the Emperor.

The Chancellor could see His Majesty was too enchanted by the warm evening to pay serious attention, and it irritated him.

They both sat beside a winding stream that flowed around and beneath the buildings of the Nine-Fold Enclosure. In the burbling, rippling water there floated little boats. Each boat held a cup of sake, or a candle, and some held little dolls dressed as nobles or fishermen. Further up and down the stream, other courtiers and ladies sat, sipping wine and writing poems that they might place on the drifting boats.

At every errant breeze, cherry blossoms fell like snow from boughs overhead, and the air was rich with their perfume. A full moon shone pale in the sky, becoming bolder as the golden-pink sunlight faded. And across the garden, hidden somewhere behind bamboo shades, Uguisu played. Her haunting melodies added poignance to the beauty of the evening, and even Daimigi found his heart tempted to drift away with her music, to float with the sake boats down the stream. And this irritated him even more.

Even so, he had kept his voice casual, hoping the Emperor might respond as a comrade, not an adversary. It would not do to break the evening's mood. "Uguisu, Your Majesty. Does she yet—"

"Oh. No, not exactly."

"What?" Daimigi immediately cursed himself for allowing his alarm to show. So long as Uguisu denied the Emperor, there remained the chance she would be sent back home as unsuitable.

"She has told me the day she will accept me."

"Indeed? And what day shall this be?"

The Emperor raised an eyebrow. "You show surprising interest in such a personal matter, Daimigi-san."

"I was merely hoping that the day would be an auspicious one."

"I'm sure it will be." The Emperor sighed and closed his eyes with a smile.

The Chancellor sighed also, but with annoyance. He dared not discuss the topic more. It disturbed him that a simple girl should prove to be such an obstacle to his plans. The guardsman had been an easy matter; he had already run away from the palace in humiliation. Things were proceeding well against the kitchen woman . . . it would take little to encourage her to leave also. Old Niwa might well die in office, aided or unaided. But Uguisu . . .

"Isn't her music beautiful?" said the Emperor. "What

an intricate melody! I cannot divine how she makes the tune do such dances."

"A pretty puzzle, Your Majesty." *Her lady-in-waiting has told me nothing useful. Still nothing is known of her mother. And all of the court loves her too much to think any ill of her.* "A pretty puzzle, indeed."

Idly, Daimigi reached out to a passing boat and snatched up the sake cup it carried. But as he tried to drink from the cup, he found instead of sake a piece of rice paper between his lips. On it some wag had written:

> "Oh dull and empty sake cup, your spirit's been
> drained dry,
> But through its magic, like the moon, now
> bright and full am I!"

Daimigi threw the poem into the water and watched as the paper danced away on the currents and eddies of the stream. He wondered if his plans, like fallen cherry blossoms and crumpled poems, were drifting away from him on the waves and currents of fortune.

By The Rasho-Mon

At the southernmost end of the Suzaku Oji, in the great crumbling wall that surrounded Heian Kyo, stood the infamous Rasho-Mon. Of all the eighteen gates to the city, the Rasho Gate had become the most reknowned. Kuma thought it ironic, as he stood leaning against one of the thick pillars, that the gate facing the direction of good fortune should attract the least fortunate of people. *Including, at the moment, myself.*

Kuma swatted at flies that hummed near his face, cursing the midafternoon heat. For a moment he wondered if it would not have been better to have remained at the palace. Soon there would be the Great Festival at the Kamo Shrine and the Procession of the Guards along the route to the shrine. Next month would come the Iris Festival, with horse races and archery contests. But staying would have meant humiliation before his comrades, and watching Katte marry someone else. *No. No, summer flies and heat are more easily endured.*

Kuma looked around at the beggars curled up asleep in the empty corners. A pair of grubby thieves conspired in their argot in an alcove. A haggard woman in patched and faded finery looked Kuma over invitingly, then assessed his probable worth and moved on. Kuma continued to stare south, down the road leading from the Rasho-Mon. He hoped, despite the heat, that there might be travelers today who would need a guide or a protector in the city.

Feeling a tug on his trousers, Kuma looked down to see a thin, dried-up stick of a beggar crouched beside him.

"Hoi, Ronin-san!"

Kuma winced at the epithet and looked away.

"Ronin-san," continued the beggar, "This is the seventh day I have seen you here. Yet you do not beg or steal. You stand as you are and wait. And I am thinking, 'What is it he is waiting for, eh?' What do you find so alluring at the Rasho-mon?" A sweep of one bony arm indicated the whole miserable structure. "Do you hope to catch a demon?"

Kuma ignored the beggar, though he was not surprised that folk tales set demons here as well as brigands.

"Ah, perhaps, I think to myself, he is waiting for a rich merchant or lord to come up the road. And this rich one will see the fine, strong man standing by the pillar and say, 'There! That is the one! He will make a perfect bodyguard!' Is that what you hope to be, Ronin-san?"

Kuma shifted in irritation. The beggar's words stung him because it was precisely what he hoped for. So far his strength had only earned him bowls of rice for chopping wood.

"Ah, I am right, I see! Well, you are in luck, Ronin-san. I am a fortune-teller. The best fortune teller in Heian Kyo. The Imperial Bureau of Divinators would have hired me, but I did not wish to work with such pompous bureaucrats. Shall I look into your future and tell you if you will become a bodyguard?"

Kuma wanted to kick the little man to send him away. But looking at the beggar's face, he saw hunger there— many hungers more than the few Kuma had suffered recently. To his surprise, Kuma felt something between sympathy and pity.

"Why do you stare at me so, Ronin-san?"

"Because I see my future in your face," Kuma said with a wry smile.

"Do you now?" The beggar grinned and struck a ridiculous pose. "A very interesting talent, that. My grandmother once claimed she could read the future in oxen droppings, and I've been told my face and they look somewhat the same. Myself, I read fortunes in gold coins." He held out an eloquent hand.

Kuma snorted. "If I had gold coins, would I be standing around here?" He made a show of searching his sleeves. Then he felt a small object in the bottom of his left sleeve. Kuma pulled out a Go-stone of the palest jade. He remembered finding it on the palace grounds. Separate from its set, it was useless. *As am I.* Kuma tossed the Go stone to the beggar. "Here, see what you can make of this."

The beggar caught the Go-stone and gaped at it. "Domo arigato, Ronin-san! This already speaks of better fortune, for me at least." Placing the Go-stone against his forehead, the beggar closed his eyes and began to sway from side to side.

Kuma sighed and leaned back against the pillar again, ignoring the beggar's theatrics.

Suddenly the beggar cried out. Kuma looked, and the thin man was staring at the Go-stone in horror. "What is the matter?" said Kuma.

"Oh, terrible!" moaned the beggar. "Terrible, terrible!" He spun around and held his head. "I see the floors of the Palace covered in blood! Many bodies! And the Emperor—Oh, horrible, horrible!"

Caught up in the beggar's words, Kuma crouched beside him and grabbed his tattered sleeve. "What do you mean, 'bodies'? Men dead? Women too? What about my Katte?"

"I don't know! I don't want to see any more!" The beggar flung down the jade Go-stone and wriggled out of Kuma's grasp. "Keep your evil talisman! I want no part of it!" Without another word, the beggar ran out of the gate, down the south road.

Kuma stood, staring after him, wondering if he should follow. Then he heard the snickers and chuckles around him.

"Well, the demons of hunger have finally taken that one's mind," said one of the thieves. "Myself, I have no prejudice against evil talismans." He quickly snatched up the jade Go-stone. Kuma grunted and waved at the thief as if to say 'go ahead, take it,' and continued staring down the road.

Through the dusty, rippling air Kuma could make out two figures approaching. They turned their heads and stared as the beggar ran by them, then continued their approach. After a minute, Kuma could see that they were priests, dressed in brown-grey robes. Kuma found this somehow reassuring after the beggar's outburst—a good omen to follow a bad one.

The thieves noticed the priests also, and huddled behind one of the pillars, conferring. As the priests came within a few yards of the Rasho Gate, the thieves trotted out to meet them.

One of the priests was an old man, the other was young. As Kuma watched, the thieves teased the elder, then began to playfully shove him. Angry that they should be harassing his good omen, Kuma ran out to them.

"Konnichi-wa, Holy Ones. Do you need a trustworthy guide into the city?" Kuma looked sidelong at the thieves and pulled his long tachi sword a hair's breadth out of its sheath.

"You shouldn't bother with these," said one of the thieves, backing off. "The old one claims they have no money, so they could not pay you."

"Then I offer my services in exchange for their prayers, which I'm sure they have in abundance."

The thieves shrugged and shuffled off, feigning nonchalance. Kuma turned to the priests, and suddenly recognized the younger one. "Takenoko!"

The young priest looked away, embarrassed.

"Takenoko, it is me—Kuma! Your old friend! What is wrong? Have you been sick? Don't you recognize me?"

"Yes, I mean, no, Kuma-san. Good afternoon to you," Takenoko said, staring at the ground.

The old priest chuckled. "Forgive him, Kuma-san. To find the holy path means leaving the world of friends and loved ones behind. Takenoko has found it hard for his feet to walk this path. He means no insult."

"Hmm." Kuma rubbed his chin, uncertain what to say.

"I'm sorry I couldn't join the palace guard," Takenoko said, "but I was so hurt by events in this world that my only thought was to leave it."

"It may be, the way things have gone, that you have made the best choice," said Kuma.

"Are things not well at the palace? Uguisu—is she all right?"

Kuma stared down the road where the beggar had gone. "I . . . I suppose." As the young priest's eyes widened, Kuma added, "The beggar you saw . . . I asked a fortune of him, and he claimed to see horrible things happening at the Palace."

The old priest chuckled. "Beggars often make dramatic pronouncements, in hope of encouraging greater charity. But since our final destination is the Imperial Palace itself, we may see for ourselves if his visions are true."

"You are going to the Palace?" said Kuma.

"Yes. We have been invited for the Washing of the Buddha and to help with preparations for the Kamo Festival. We will not need a guide, Kuma-san. But if you will see us through this gate, then you will certainly have earned our prayers."

"Then it is my honor to do so," said Kuma, bowing.

Together the three of them walked silently through the gate, feeling the eyes of its wretched denizens upon them. A few yards on the other side, standing in the Suzaku Oji, Kuma asked, "Are you sure you will not need a guide further?"

The old priest said, "Since our final destination is straight down this avenue, I think not."

Kuma shifted uneasily. "In that case . . . Takenoko, will you take a message there for me?"

"Certainly, Kuma, if I can."

"See if the Myobu Katte-san is all right, will you? And if you see her, tell her . . . tell her I am well. That is all. And give her some orange blossoms from the garden."

"I will try, Kuma-san. But Katte is a Myobu now?"

"Much has changed since you left, Takenoko. You will see." *But I hope you see nothing like whatever the beggar saw.*

"Thank you for your guidance, Kuma-san," said the old priest. "We shall remember you in our prayers, as we agreed."

As the priests walked away down the avenue, Kuma said softly, "Yes, pray for me, Takenoko. Pray for us all."

The Chancellor's Gift

The Myobu Katte sat alone by the blinds in a large room. She felt as though she would melt into the tatami mat beneath her, the heat was so oppressive. Though the blinds beside her had been raised halfway, no cooling breezes came in from the garden outside. The dainty fan she held was scarcely any help. Her kimonos, though unlined and of the sheerest silk gossamer, clung damp and heavy against her skin. It seemed all she could do to sit motionless and breathe the hot, humid air.

The Palace around her was eerily silent, except for the high-pitched twitter of cicadas and occasional distant footsteps. Nearly everyone had gone to the Kamo Festival at the Upper Kamo Shrine. Usually the most impressive ceremony of the year, this year it would be greater still. The Emperor's eldest daughter was being installed as the High Priestess of the Shrine, and everyone of quality felt obligated to make an appearance.

Katte's ladies had all insisted upon going, of course. But they had made dark hints that the kami of the shrine, as well as some attendees, might take offense if one of lowly birth were to "play at being noble" and attend. Katte had allowed them to believe it was their words that had cowed her into staying behind. In fact, she had her own reasons.

At midday the palace guards had begun their procession to the Lower Kamo Shrine, escorting the carriages of the nobility. Katte remembered how she used to peek out from the kitchens when the guards assembled in the courtyard, and how thrilled she would be at finding Kuma's proud face in the company. But today, though she could have ridden in a grand carriage in the very midst of the procession, Kuma's face would not be there to look for. And so, it seemed to her, there was no point in going.

Katte sighed and fanned herself a little more. Her family had told her to forget Kuma, but she could not. And then the monk with Kuma's message had arrived. Though she had been pleased that he had not been banished for some unspeakable crime, as some had rumored it, the message had fueled her dissatisfaction.

Poor Kuma. In that horrid place, the Rasho-Mon. If only I could go to him, I would leave this place in a moment! It was a foolish, selfish fantasy, she knew. Her once poor family now depended on her income of rice and gold. Her ailing mother was finally showing signs of improving health. For Katte to leave her position would doom her family to poverty once more, and her mother to certain death. But she paid little interest in their efforts to find her a noble husband. That was a fate she preferred not to think about.

Katte's thoughts were suddenly disturbed by the loud thudding of approaching feet—a man's stride—along the veranda just outside her blinds. As Katte held her breath, the man stopped as he came up beside her.

"Lady Katte? Someone told me you were still here, but

I was not sure I should believe them. May I speak with you a moment?"

The Chancellor! Why would he wish to speak to me? Katte could imagine how her ladies would have dashed about, frantically trying to set things properly, were they here. Katte found herself adjusting her robes and smoothing her hair self-consciously, even though Daimigi could not see her. "Of course, Your Excellency," she said. She slid a cushion beneath the blinds to him and started to roll the blinds fully down.

The Chancellor's hand caught her sleeve. "There is no need to hide yourself further, my lady. I am hardly likely to come crawling into your room in this weather. But tell me, why are you not at the Festival?"

"I . . . I was feeling ill this morning, Your Excellency. I felt it would be unwise to attend."

"I see. Yes, I had heard you have not been feeling well. But I am most interested in hearing how you are faring in your new position."

Katte wondered what rumors had reached him. Her ladies would often receive messages for her, then insist upon writing the replies themselves. Katte could barely write, so that was reasonable. But often they would not even show her what they had written. For all Katte knew, terrible things might be attributed to her. Considering the snobbishness of her ladies, in fact, Katte thought it quite likely. "Things are . . . things are well, Your Excellency."

"Indeed? I had heard that life is not as easy for you as it should be. Please feel free to tell me if anything troubles your heart. I am responsible for the good operation of the Palace and Administration. Is there anything I may do for you?"

His kind words touched Katte and threatened to bring

tears she thought were well buried. "I . . . well, some things have been . . . difficult."

"Ah. Yes, life at Court can be trying, even for those of us who are born to position here. I have heard stories of women from common background who are treated terribly when they come to Court. It is most shameful. I hope you are given due respect and dignity."

Katte started to reply, but found no words for her feelings. Part of her wanted to blurt out her true situation. Yet she felt it would not be seemly to whine and complain to this noble lord.

"Is it so bad then?" said the Chancellor, apparently understanding her silence. "Dear me, I had hoped the rumors were false. Is there some way I can be of assistance? There is little men can do in women's affairs, I know, but please suggest whatever might help you. Shall I have your ladies-in-waiting assigned to another household?"

Only to have them hate me further? And to give me a new set of aloof maidservants? "I am sorry, Your Excellency, I do not think that would be helpful."

"No? I understand. Unbiased ladies would be terribly difficult to find. I can see your difficulty. Your family relies upon your work here, do they not? So you are unable to leave then if conditions become unbearable. Most unfortunate. But I wish to demonstrate that at least one soul at Court is concerned for you. Please accept this gift from me. It is a small token of kindness, I know, but I feel I should do something for you. It is your own choice what to do with it, but I know you will choose wisely."

Katte watched, bewildered, as Daimigi pushed a beautiful box of carved Shen wood under the blinds. "Oh, no, Your Excellency, I could not possibly—"

"Please, it is but a humble gift. All I ask is that you do

not tell anyone at Court that it was I who gave it to you. There is no need to give anyone another excuse for spreading malicious gossip."

"Of course, Your Excellency. Thank you so very much."

"You are quite welcome. And now I must attend to other important business before I return to the Kamo Shrine. Sayonara, Myobu Katte."

"Good day to you, Your Excellency." As she heard him rise and stride away, Katte pulled the box closer and lifted its lid. Within it lay a bundle of blue silk. Katte pulled aside the corners of the silk wrapping and gasped at what was revealed. In the box lay twelve bars of gold . . . more than she would earn in years of service. Katte closed the box and wept in gratitude.

Iris Festival

It was the nightmare again, Uguisu knew. There was the same, dull golden light, darkening toward the edges as if she were looking through an ancient bronze mirror. Within this light she saw the same face—an infant with eyes intelligent far beyond his age, leering up at her as he suckled at her breast. The light rippled as if it were a reflection in troubled water, and there came a new scene. A boy child, barely able to stand, stood watching something moving on the floor while he laughed. Uguisu was unable to keep herself from looking at the floor, though she knew what she would see. There the Emperor lay, moaning and writhing in the throes of poisoned death. And the little prince laughed, playing with the cup from which the Emperor had just drunk.

Hands gripped her arms, and Uguisu opened her eyes. She found herself sitting up on her sleeping mat, and her mouth was open. Uguisu knew, because it had happened before, that she had been screaming.

"My Lady!" wailed Nikao, "Are you all right? What is the matter?"

"It was bad dreams again, neh?" said Shonasaki. "What demons torment you so?"

"Do not speak like that!" Nikao said. "This is a day of evil aspect, when angry spirits may roam the earth! Do not attract them with such talk!"

And this is the day I am to receive my Emperor, thought Uguisu bitterly.

"I know well what day it is, Nikao. My lady, there are still priests at the Palace who have remained from the Kamo Festival. One of them is said to be skilled at exorcism. Would you like to speak to him?"

"No, thank you," said Uguisu. "I do not need an exorcist." *Not yet.* She rose and the ladies helped her dress.

The morning passed ever so slowly, as the ladies adorned the eaves and doorways of their quarters with garlands of iris leaves and sprigs of sage branches, taking down the hare sticks that had been hung on New Year's Day. They placed iris flowers in their hair, and adorned their Chinese jackets with azalea and orange blossoms. They gave pillows stuffed with iris and sage to friends and servants.

Palace guardsmen could be heard passing by, carrying leaves and branches wherever needed. Women from the Bureau of the Imperial Wardrobe delivered herbal balls decorated with braided multi-colored string. These were hung on the pillars at each corner of each room. By midday, the entire palace grounds looked like an enormous hanging garden, and all the people in it like strange, wandering flower bushes.

Kitsune and Nikao laughed gaily, and Shonasaki wrote one poem after another. Uguisu felt numb inside. But she was not upset that the hours seemed so long. She wished there could be an eternity between that morning and the evening to come.

The afternoon was filled with archery contests and horse races and other manly competitions that the ladies watched from behind bamboo curtains. It was said that such displays of virile strength helped keep the evil spirits at bay. Uguisu imagined her guardian spirit laughing heartily at that.

The Emperor himself presided over the contests, offering wine in which iris leaves had been steeped to the winners and to the noble lords. Uguisu hoped his duties might cause him to forget her, but at the Hour of the Monkey she received a poem from him:

> "Today Heaven is a garden blossoming with hope,
> Today, even the ancient pine tree wears lavender."

"Lavender," Shonasaki explained, "is the color of romantic liaisons. And of course, the 'ancient pine' is himself, who has been waiting a long time. And Heaven could mean both the Imperial Palace and himself."

So he has certainly not forgotten, thought Uguisu.

From behind the blinds, she watched the Emperor as he gave the awards to the winning guards. How kind and generous he seemed, how sensitive and noble. *How can an ancient need for revenge claim the life of such as he? It does not seem just. How can I do what is asked of me?* But another part of her mind answered, *It is for the honor of your family that you do this. For the mother who taught you and gave her life for you. For your grandmother and all of the mothers before her whose efforts led to you and this moment. Seven generations of debt do you owe.* Uguisu felt the weight of those generations press upon her heart like stones. She remembered something her mother once said; "The important thing in life is not a whim of the heart. The important thing is duty. It is the duty of the men of a clan to defend its honor. It is the duty of its women to bear its children." *Even*, thought Uguisu, *when the child born is unnatural, a creature possessed?*

After the contests and awards ended, there was, as at all festivals, a great banquet. But this time, Uguisu was not asked to play music for it. Instead, she was taken by her ladies-in-waiting to a special room in the Seriyō Den. There her ladies dressed her in three loose kimonos of the sheerest white silk that had been scented with a delicate perfume. Her thick raven hair was combed again and again, and allowed to flow freely over her shoulders and down to her knees. The ladies bustled about the room, adjusting the kicho, cushions and reed mats to be just so. Nikao could not seem to keep from giggling. Uguisu wanted to slap her.

Instead, summoning what control she could, Uguisu said the line she had been rehearsing in her mind all day. "Please, could you remove some of the iris and sage from the north doorway? My nose has become quite irritated from their scent, and I would like the breeze blowing in off the veranda to be fresh. One wouldn't want to sneeze while the Emperor is visiting."

This sent Nikao into new gales of laughter. "Why, no! Then he might think your love is false."

"But what of evil spirits?" asked Shonasaki.

Kitsune clucked, "You would almost make me think you believed in such things!"

"I would think," said Uguisu, "that if my Lord of Heaven is not sufficiently powerful to drive away evil spirits, there would be little hope for our Empire."

"Oh, beautifully said!" Nikao exclaimed, clapping her hands.

"If that is what you truly wish," said Shonasaki. She obligingly removed some of the iris leaves from the blind facing the north veranda. Then the ladies arranged the kicho carefully around Uguisu, bowed their "good evenings" to her and withdrew.

Uguisu felt utterly alone in the darkening twilight gloom. She became aware of a growing excitement within her, anticipating the Emperor's warm embrace. Yet her heart ached, knowing the price he would someday pay for this evening of pleasure with her. The leering eyes of the demon-child in her nightmares drifted again through her mind.

She looked around at the objects near her kicho, wanting to fill her sight with anything but the evil face she saw. Her gaze settled on a tiny bonsai pine, a gift from the Emperor—a symbol of his willingness to wait for her. *He has been so kind. Other men, such as Hidoi, would have wheedled, demanded or forced their way through to me. Must I repay his kindness with treachery? Though one has duty to one's family, is there not also duty to one's husband, lord and emperor?*

She sat many minutes just feeling herself breathe. The only sounds in her awareness were the high-pitched drone of the cicadas outside, and the beating of her heart. It seemed, as she waited, that the pounding was becoming louder, until she realized it was the sound of approaching footsteps. She heard the shoji slide open and cultured voices softly wishing one a pleasant evening as they departed. Then the shoji slid shut and someone approached the kicho. The Emperor had arrived.

"Uguisu?" His voice was low and gentle.

Uguisu swallowed and tried to return a greeting, but her throat felt suddenly tight and she could say nothing.

His hand appeared at the edge of the kicho-frame and slowly drew it aside. Uguisu dared not look up at his face, but she could see the edge of his gold silk robe, and catch the scent of its elegant perfume. Her awareness of his nearness was overpowering and she felt transfixed, unable to move.

His hand gently caressed her cheek, and he said, "You are very beautiful, Uguisu."

His loving words made her keenly feel her shame, and she found she still could not speak.

Gently, the Emperor pulled aside the folds of her kimonos, until she was partially revealed to him. He ran his hand ever so lightly down the nape of her neck, her shoulder, under the curve of her small breast. Uguisu's breathing became quick and shallow, and her heart fluttered like hummingbird wings. Slowly the Emperor moved to embrace her.

"No!" Uguisu shrieked, flinging herself out of the Emperor's arms. Pulling the kicho around her, she said, "No, you mustn't! You mustn't touch me! Go away! Go far from me, oh please, please!"

For long moments, her sobbing was the only sound.

Then she heard the Emperor ask softly, "Is it because I am old, Uguisu, that you reject me so?"

She could hear the hurt and disappointment in his voice, and it was like a knife in her heart. "No, you do not understand. I cannot tell you. I am ... I am unworthy, my lord. I would bring you bad fortune. Please, send me away. Forget me. But you mustn't touch me!"

She heard him sigh and there were more long moments of silence. Then she heard him rise, and, with slow, weary step, leave the room without another word.

Uguisu huddled, shaking, for she did not know how many moments. Then she heard a rising wind outside.

Louder it grew, moaning and whistling through the blinds. Suddenly, with a snap, the blind was blown open and a great gust of wind blew the kicho aside.

The blind flapped in the gale, and Uguisu could see in the sky a huge grey storm cloud boiling and darkening. Its folds and billows began to form into the shape of a face, and with terror Uguisu realized it was the face of her guardian spirit scowling down at her.

"Betrayer! Traitor! You should not have disobeyed, Uguisu!" the wind howled and hissed.

Uguisu grabbed at the few nearby herbal balls and iris leaves and clutched them tightly to her chest, gasping with fright.

"Those will not protect you long," the wind moaned. "You will be punished for your treachery! You and your precious Emperor. You think you have saved him, but you have not. Our vengeance on the Fujiwara will yet be realized, despite you. You will see, Uguisu. You have won nothing! You will see."

Lightning flashed and thunder rumbled as the dark cloud roiled and changed shape, becoming the face of a bearded man with intense eyes. Uguisu had seen those eyes before, in her dreams. "Cursed are you, treacherous child!" roared the wind, "Cursed is your flesh that will suffer torment. Cursed is your spirit that shall wander the earth without end when you are dust! Remember this and know that you have brought this upon yourself."

With another crash of thunder, the bamboo blind slammed back across the doorway, and Uguisu trembled alone in the howling dark.

Changing Paths

"We have lost, Mother. The treacherous girl has defeated us."

"No, Nagaya-chan, do not be such a nay-sayer. We had placed all our hopes upon one bridge that proved faulty and crumbled. This does not mean there are no other paths to our goal."

"We may yet do damage to the Fujiwara, yes. But I will not have the body of a prince to enter. I will not be reborn as Emperor."

"Do not be so certain even of that, my son. The Emperor must have an heir, and therefore an Empress. Perhaps even the Chancellor's daughter. Now wouldn't that be sweet irony?"

"But I may not freely enter a babe that is not of my blood. To do so requires intricate ritual that can only be performed by one of flesh and substance."

"Even that might yet be arranged, never fear. We shall see. Let me think."

Hot Winds

Netsubo left the noise of the chanting and gongs of the Shinto priests behind as he strode into the Plum Pavillion. Having decided that his presence was not necessary to have his "sins and impurities" purged from his soul, he did not think the gathering of noblemen and officials at the Great Gate of the Imperial Palace would notice his absence. Netsubo had chosen this opportunity for a more important task.

The lady-in-waiting called Shonasaki approached him, eyes properly cast down, saying, "How are we honored by your presence, Lord of the Household?"

"I wish to speak to my daughter Uguisu."

"If you please, sir, she is observing a day of abstinence, as are many in the palace. It is her duty to observe the strictures—"

"And it is the duty of a daughter to speak to her father when he commands it! You will prepare her to see me at once!"

"But My Lord, it will nullify the purifying aspects of the abs—"

"She has done enough to 'nullify its aspects'! Will I see her, or will I have you replaced with a more obedient maid?"

"As you wish, My Lord," Shonasaki said softly. "Wait but a moment."

Netsubo listened to the irritating rustle of her kimonos as the lady-in-waiting hurried away. He tried to calm himself, fanning the close, muggy air from his face. He did not wish in any way to appear an incompetent father. It seemed many long moments before the lady-in-waiting returned.

"She is ready, my lord."

Netsubo was ushered into a bare room, dominated by a large, plain black kicho that bore many ivory prayer tags on its frame. To his consternation, several Buddhist monks were kneeling in one corner, reading softly from scrolls they held.

"What is this, Uguisu? Shouldn't these be out at the gate for the ceremony?"

"If you please, father, the Purification rites are Shinto. It would not be seemly. And I need them here to guide my troubled spirit."

"Hmpf. Shinto and Buddhist mix often enough. And you would be better guided by common sense."

"Please, father—"

"I had hoped I could say what I have to say to you alone. Do you think I do not know what the rumors say about you? About *me*? Have you any idea what will happen to us if you continue in this foolish behavior?"

"You do not understand, father! There are things you do not know."

"No, there are things you do not know! Like how to behave as a grown woman instead of a child!"

"Father, I am afraid of—"

"Yes, you are afraid. Where has all your courage flown, eh? Why can you not accept your responsibilities? He is the Emperor, Uguisu! Have you forgotten?"

"No, father. All I have done . . ." Her voice trailed off into sobs.

"All you have done will gain you nothing, if he becomes displeased with you. What if I am sent off again as governor of some far province, eh? Who will listen to your pretty flute then? Surely your ancestors would look down on you in shame."

There was silence behind the kicho, then the sound of rustling paper. "There is a message I must give you, father. A very important message." Her voice caught as if breaking off a sob. "It explains why I have behaved this way. You may read it, so you will understand me better. But the message is intended for the Fujiwara Chancellor."

"And what would you have to say to the Chancellor that is so important?"

"Please do not ask me now, father. I know you speak to Daimigi-sama often. You are the best person to take him this message. He will listen to you." A large piece of folded, heavy Michoku paper was slid to him from beneath the kicho. "Please see that he gets it soon. He must be warned."

"Warned! What can you possibly mean?"

But there came only the sound of quiet weeping behind the curtain.

Netsubo sighed. "I see it is no use speaking to you like this. Think well on my words, Uguisu. Remember, it is your duty to obey." He stood to go, then noticed the face of a young monk who quickly turned away. *He is familiar somehow.*

Netsubo stepped out of the room and heard the shoji slide shut behind him. Rapidly he walked down the corridor and out of the building. He paused on the stairs and wondered at Uguisu's stubbornness. Pulling open the folded note she had given him, Netsubo read:

To His Most August Excellency, Chancellor Fujiwara no Daimigi, from the Lady Uguisu. Through the kind efforts of my father, Minister of the Imperial Household Echizen no Netsubo, I send you greetings and warnings. It is with deepest regret and utmost urgency that I must advise you that your family and His Imperial Majesty are in the gravest danger. There are powerful evil spirits who seek revenge upon the Fujiwara for a long-past injustice. These spirits have used me to gain entrance to the Palace. My strange behavior has been for the purpose of denying them greater power in our world, but I fear I may only have delayed them. Please take all precautions to defend yourself, your family, and His Majesty against evil spirits and demons. And please hold my father blameless for this. The fault is entirely my own. Please keep yourself and His Majesty well.

"Evil spirits and demons?" muttered Netsubo. "Has she gone mad? Is that why she keeps those priests around her?" He remembered the face of the familiar-looking priest, and recognition struck him like a blow. *Takenoko! The son of that creature Niwa. The one Uguisu . . . could it be? Could it be that she rejects the Emperor because her former love has returned? Has she taken up with him again, even though he is a monk?! And she keeps him brazenly by her with pretense of piety, and false warnings of evil spirits! Well, she will receive no assistance from me in her little scheme! I will not let her embarrass me this way.*

Netsubo tore the note into many small pieces and flung them into the air. The paper floated and drifted far over the Plum Palace courtyard, unseasonal snowflakes on the hot wind.

Night of the Weaver

"It is clouding over," said Shonasaki, gazing through the blinds at the late summer evening sky.

"Oh, I hope we do not have another storm," said Nikao. "Not one like the Iris Festival storm, when Our Lady. . . ." Nikao looked down at her hands.

"These do not seem to be storm clouds," said Shonasaki. "Though it may rain a little."

"So," said Kitsune, "the heavenly magpies will not make their bridge across the sky, and the Weaver and the Herdsman stars must wait another year before they meet again."

Shonasaki sighed. "It seems a season of ill-aspect for lovers meeting."

"That is foolishness," said Kitsune. "Lady Uguisu rejected the Emperor by her own choice—"

"But why?" whispered Shonasaki.

"—and Kazenatsu has been very . . . attentive to me."

"So long as you tell him about the doings of Our Lady," said Shonasaki.

"It isn't like that!" Kitsune snapped. "And besides, I am only looking after all our interests. Our Lady must be mad to treat the Emperor so! She is very fortunate he hasn't sent her away."

"Kitsune!" Nikao complained, "you mustn't speak of the Lady we serve that way!"

"Oh, mustn't I? Even when her behavior hurts the Emperor and endangers us all? What will become of us when His Majesty at last tires of her rudeness? When she is sent away, will you follow her and continue to serve? Even if she is sent up the Tokkaido to the island of hairy savages?"

Nikao looked down and said nothing.

"I might," said Shonasaki.

"You are too romantic and impractical," said Kitsune.

"That is why her poems are so nice," Nikao said softly.

"And does your heart always follow the practical path, Kitsune?" said Shonasaki.

"Well, at least I don't believe in ghosts," she replied, looking pointedly at Nikao.

"I tell you I saw them! An old woman and a man with a rope around his neck!"

"Indeed," clucked Kitsune.

"Leave her be," said Shonasaki.

"Me? It was you who put those foolish ideas in her head!"

"Foolish? Do you believe in nothing beyond what your eyes can see? There is an evil atmosphere about the Palace these days. Can you not feel it?"

"Stop it!" Kitsune snapped.

"Let's talk about something else," Nikao said anxiously.

For a moment they sat in silence.

"What was that argument you and Kazenatsu were having the other morning?" Shonasaki asked slyly.

"It wasn't an argument," said Kitsune. "It was a . . . discussion."

"A disagreement, then. Well?"

"He merely wanted to know what sort of present I would like, as he wanted to give me one. I said that a man of such position should be able to get the best monotagari, and that is what I would like."

"Monotagari?" said Nikao.

"Romance stories," said Shonasaki.

"Kazenatsu laughed at me and asked how I could read such silly things. But I told him that they are beautiful stories. Ladies have been reading and writing them for many years. They are much more interesting than the stilted works of Chinese scholars that he reads."

"And you say my nature is too romantic."

"It's not the same thing!"

"Let's not get back into that, please?" said Nikao. "Have each of you prayed to the Weaver tonight? I lit incense to her and asked that She help my sewing improve. Have you asked Her for anything, Kitsune?"

Kitsune blushed. "Not anything I would tell you about."

"Shonasaki? Did you ask Her for help with your poetry?"

"No. I asked Her to help Our Lady. And the Emperor."

"That is kind of you. I suppose Lady Uguisu has asked for help in music."

"She does not need help in music," Kitsune grumbled. "She needs good sense."

"It is so strange," said Shonasaki. "It is nearly autumn and the joy we hoped for a year ago still eludes us." Taking up brush and inkstone, she wrote on a piece of yellow paper:

"The summer maple leaf reddens on the bough,
Who knows which way the autumn storms will blow?"

Autumn

秋

A bare black tree,
A black crow takes early rest,
Against autumn twilight.
            —Bashō

OLD NIWA

WAITING ON THE VERANDA outside his father's sickroom, Takenoko watched the gentle rain as it hissed and pattered against the roof and leaves. *As if Heaven itself weeps.* The cool, damp air was fragrant with the scent of chrysanthemums. Takenoko thought this rudely ironic. Vain noblemen and women would leave long pieces of silk floss draped over the flowers to catch the "chrysanthemum dew" of autumn mornings. They would then rub the damp, aromatic cloth over their bodies, believing that this would prevent the effects of aging. Takenoko doubted the fragrant rain mist could do anything to help his father now.

Before long, a lady-in-waiting admitted him through the blinds and he entered the room. Though, outside, he had felt only cool acceptance, the sight of his father lying ill brought hot tears to Takenoko's cheeks. Old Niwa lay swathed in his voluminous black robes of office, incense burners smoking at the head and foot of his sleeping mat. The skin of his face and hands seemed waxy and pale, and he appeared shrunken within his robes. Only his narrow, black eyes retained most of their former light. "Welcome, my son," he said softly. "You will forgive old Niwa if he cannot greet you properly, neh?"

This brought from Takenoko only a sob instead of a reply. He hung his head, finding the sight of what his father had become too painful to view. This also moved the four ladies-in-waiting who attended Niwa, and they had to wipe the tears from their faces with their somber grey sleeves. "There, now, girls," Niwa said, "do not make such noise. This is not yet a funeral. Be off with you if you cannot control yourselves."

The ladies rose and slowly trooped to the shoji, slipping out with sad looks back at old Niwa. After they left, Niwa said with a dry chuckle, "They even dress in grey robes of mourning, though I am not yet dead."

"It is rude of them," Takenoko managed to say.

"Ah, now, my son, I should not see tears from you. It is unseemly for monks to cry. Though if you had stayed with me, and become a court nobleman, you might cry all you like. You should see them, Takenoko. These Gentlemen Who Dwell Among the Clouds will shed tears like rain at the drop of a cherry blossom."

"You are right, father. I should have stayed with you. I should not have left you to . . . this!"

"No, my son. I believe you made the best choice. If you knew the pettiness and nastiness that goes on, the triviality and boredom of noble life . . . no, the Path to Heaven is surely better. It cheers me that I myself might take that path before long," Niwa added, coughing and shifting uncomfortably on his sleeping mat.

"You mustn't talk like that!" said Takenoko. "This is only a minor illness. You must get better!"

"Polite lies from a monk?" Niwa chided. "My son, you were to have left such concern for me well behind you on your path, were you not?"

"I . . . I have found that path hard, father. I find I cannot leave some things behind."

"Ah," said Niwa. "Ah." Carefully propping himself up on one elbow, Niwa frowned and said softly, "There are rumors, Takenoko, most dangerous ones. Have you not left Uguisu behind on your path?"

"She is hardest to leave behind, father. Especially now that I serve her in prayer."

"These rumors, Takenoko, say that you serve her in other ways as well."

Takenoko gasped and blanched.

"My son, the penalty for interfering with an imperial lady is banishment. If Uguisu is to become Empress, it would be instant execution."

Takenoko clenched his fists and struck the floor. "But I have done nothing! Nothing that could be thought as such!"

"Please, my son, you know these walls are paper."

More softly, Takenoko went on. "You don't know how often, as I have knelt chanting beside her kicho, I have ached to give her a note, a poem, some indication it was I who prayed for her. But I have not! I even change my voice when I am near her so she will not guess. She does not even know I'm there! Please believe me, father, those rumors are but wind!"

Niwa sighed. "I believe you. I know you to be a good

lad. Let us hope those in power believe so too. For, if they do not, I doubt I shall be around to defend you."

"Don't talk like that! If there was some way I could prove my loyalty to the Emperor—"

"Such action might be regarded with suspicion, unless it comes to you naturally. You cannot command blossoms to grow so that you may pick them. You must wait for their own time, then take them as they appear. My advice to you is to leave the Palace, if you can. Give no more cause for gossip. Then return when you can be of better service to the Emperor. Or return to your mountain temple and live the proper life of a monk."

"I cannot leave you, father. Not like this."

"There is no more you can do for me, my son. I have done all that needed doing in my life and I am now ready to face its end. I probably should have turned to holy study myself, but you will add to my karma for this life. My next shall surely be better because of you."

"Can I give you no more service in this life? Could I not call in my master to drive out the demon of illness that besets you?"

"No demon causes this illness. At least, not a demon of the spiritual sort."

"What do you mean?"

Niwa waved a limp hand. "Tsk. Just the suspicions of a sick old man. No, my body is possessed only by age. And any attempts to remove that from me would only hasten my passage from this life. No, Takenoko, there is no more you can do, except to follow my advice and go. Find your Path to Heaven. I shall not be far behind you." Niwa settled back within his robes and relaxed, drifting off into sleep.

Takenoko hesitated, fearing that his father might never

wake from his sleep. But, at last, he murmured a short blessing over Niwa's still form, and walked back out into the whispering rain.

O-Bon Visitor

Netsubo tossed and turned on his sleeping mat. Elsewhere in the palace there were Bon-fires crackling and people dancing for the dead. Their wailing songs and the pounding of their drums were all too audible to the sleepless Household Minister.

Netsubo had had no wish to speak to his ancestors or other relatives who had passed on. He had no wish to share with them the humiliation he was suffering in court. So he had contrived to absent himself from the O-Bon festivities. He had asked the Imperial Bureau of Divination for a favor in exchange for some better furnishings for their office. They obliged him, stating that because of yin-this and yang-that and the coincidence of the Day of the Monkey with the time of the Little Brother of Metal, it would be bad luck for him to go anywhere, and particularly to interact with the dead. So Netsubo gladly had performed the necessary ablutions and put himself to bed. And lay there, sleepless.

He huddled more beneath his sleeping robes and tried to shut out the noises from outside. Suddenly, he felt his feet become chilled, as if they had touched soft snow. Looking up, he was shocked to see his dead wife, Uguisu's mother, standing at the foot of his mat. She was as beautiful as he remembered her, and for a moment he felt disoriented in time. Then he noticed her face was unnaturally pale. And her light grey kimonos ended in wisps like smoke that trailed away from her . . . well above the floor. "D-dearest wife!"

"Netsu-chan." Her voice was sad and distant.

"Why have you come to me? I did not summon you."

"We do not always need a summons to appear, dear husband. Particularly on O-Bon night. I have come at the call of others."

"What others?"

But she ignored his question. The cold, trailing wisps of her robes brushed his ankles, and Netsubo jerked his feet beneath himself and sat up. "I have worried about you, Netsu-chan," she said at last, sighing.

"Worried? Why should you worry about me, dearest? Have I not attained an important position in the Imperial Palace? Our beautiful daughter has—"

"Our daughter has betrayed us, Netsu-chan."

Netsubo hung his head and sighed. *So it was no use trying to hide from the dead.* "Yes. But what can I do? I would disown her, yet I dare not so long as the Emperor gives any shred of support to her. And for some foolish reason, His Majesty seems reluctant to give her up. I have, at least, arranged for those monks who attend her to be sent away. I would have forced them out sooner, but Uguisu made such a scene about needing them by her tonight that it would have been most embarrassing to press matters."

"You did what was proper, my husband. But there is more you can do."

"More?"

"I worry for you and the position you have worked so hard to obtain. I hurt at the way our selfish daughter's transgressions may harm you. I feel, in part, responsible. I was, perhaps, too lenient a mother."

"Nonsense. You were a perfect mother! It is my fault. I did not keep an eye on her as I should and allowed her to become willful."

"It is a willful child indeed who disobeys her guardians," said the ghost, her voice taking on a steely edge. "Yet, I would at least help you, beloved, so that you might escape the consequences of her misbehavior. There is something you can do to remain in the Emperor's favor."

"What is that, dearest wife?"

"Listen. I shall tell you . . ."

The Chinese Courtesan

The Emperor sat in a large, sumptuous audience room in the Chancellor's Palace suite, feeling more unsettled than he had ever felt in his life. He found it difficult to pay attention to the noblemen around him, the fourteen sumo wrestlers who kneeled before him, or the Chancellor who was gesturing at them and saying,

"I thought we'd do things a little differently this year, Your Majesty. You may select seven from these who will be the 'Chrysanthemum Team.' Those who are left will be the 'Wisteria Team.' That should be much more interesting than merely calling them teams of the Left and Right, don't you think?"

"Hmmm?" The Emperor heard Uguisu, hidden in the back of the room behind a bamboo screen, take up a mournful tune. The Emperor had often wondered, of late, why he did not simply send her away. *Hope?* he thought, *that she might change her mind? I certainly owe nothing to the cold, ungrateful little—* He caught himself in midthought, as her music soared into a flight of shuddering, sighing melody that spoke of hopes unrealized. *Her music so well matches my mood. As if our souls were once very close . . . perhaps in a former life. Perhaps that is why I cannot bear to part with her.*

"Your Majesty?" Daimigi prompted.

"What? Oh. Yes. Quite so." He waved his golden fan at seven wrestlers at random, saying, "Him," and "That one," and "You'll do." The Emperor wondered at how quickly he had lost control of things. Old Niwa lay gravely ill, his duties now taken by his deputy—a Fujiwara, of course. The Myobu Katte had suddenly resigned her position. The guard Kuma had left under a cloud of scandal. *The allies I had hoped to gather around me have fallen one by one. And Uguisu . . .*

"Your Majesty! Are you well?"

"What? Oh, I am fine, Daimigi-san. I was merely thinking of . . . a poem. Yes, those seven will do fine." But a very strange poem Uguisu had sent him would not leave his mind. She had written:

> "Avenging winds will scourge the flowered
> > > meadow.
> And shred the clouds of Heaven as they pass,
> When poor men's houses are allowed within
> > > the palace,
> The wise man wears the iris all the year."

Below the poem had been written the words "Please protect yourself." Folded within the note had been another piece of white paper on which was written a prayer to one's ancestors.

The Emperor could not make any sense of it. The first line could refer to the Fujiwara, whose name meant 'wisteria plain.' *But the rest . . . Why did she use the odd word 'nagaya' to refer to houses, and why would they appear in the Palace?* The Emperor sighed and shook his head. *Could it be the rumors that she is mad are true? They say she is mortally afraid of spirits, not to mention her fear of me. And what of the rumor that one of the monks she kept near her is her former lover, and might be again? I cannot, in my heart, believe that. And I do not think her mad. Her poem is a warning, clearly, but of what or whom?* Looking at all the noblemen in the room, he thought, *Is it one of you?*

"—and we offer Your August and Most High Majesty, upon whose shoulders shines the golden light of Heaven, our most sincere and humble gratitude."

The Emperor realized it was one of the sumo he had chosen who spoke, and the seven selected all slowly touched their foreheads to the floormats.

"How I envy your strength," the Emperor murmured.

The sumo who had spoken before said, "Surely, Great Majesty, our strength is nothing compared to the might of your imperial power."

The Emperor exhaled a sardonic "Heh!" which he swiftly covered with a cough. "Well, yes. Of course."

He noticed Daimigi giving him a momentary frown. Then the Chancellor waved his fan, saying, "You may return to your training."

"Yes," the Emperor added, "I look forward to seeing your efforts."

The wrestlers bowed once more and rose. Uguisu played a sprightly saibara from the southern provinces and some of the sumo sang along as they waddled out of the hall.

"Must she always be playing, Your Majesty?" said the Chancellor, gesturing with his fan towards Uguisu.

"No, you are right. She may need a rest." The Emperor called a page boy to him. "Tell the Lady Uguisu she may retire to her quarters." The little page scurried off.

Moments later, Uguisu's music stopped, and the Emperor felt the same odd emptiness as every other time she stopped. He heard the rustling of her stiff court kimonos as she was led away and, in a room full of courtiers, he felt alone.

"Your Majesty," Daimigi said softly, leaning closer, "I was wondering if this evening we might have a discussion of a private matter of some importance."

"Your daughter." The Emperor tiredly rubbed his brows.

"Yes, in fact. Time passes on, and I have had no reply from you. Her mother and I are wondering if we should wait for offers from others. But it is you I am worried for, Your Majesty. You can afford to wait far less than she."

Yes, thought the Emperor, *Time passes on, and I am still without heir, without true friends, without allies, without love. Perhaps even taking a girl-child to my heart would be better than this . . . emptiness.* "Very well, Daimigi-san. Bring your daughter to the Seriyō Den this evening and we shall plan the wedding."

For a brief moment, the Emperor beheld on Daimigi's face a victorious smile, that was broken as a little page rushed back into the hall.

Flinging his forehead to the floor, the page cried, "Your Majesty, Lord Netsubo of the Imperial Household craves an urgent word with you!"

"What does he want?" grumbled the Emperor.

"He says it is most important that he speak to Your Majesty right away!"

"Very well, show him in."

Netsubo entered in a rush, nearly knocking over the little page boy. He knelt before the Emperor and pressed his forehead to the floor. "Thank you, Most Gracious Majesty, for agreeing to see this most unworthy servant."

Now what could be bothering him? "As one of my more valued advisors, Netsubo-san," the Emperor replied politely, "you know I always find your advice important. What have you to tell us?" Netsubo sat up, nervous excitement in his eyes. "Oh mighty Emperor, as keeper of the

Imperial Household, it is my honor to see that you receive a gift for you that has arrived at the Palace."

"I see. But why doesn't the giver of the gift present it
himself?"

"Because the giver is far away, Your Majesty, and his
agents may not enter the Palace."

The Emperor frowned in confusion. "And who might
be this generous, but distant benefactor?"

"If it please Your Majesty, the gift is from His Imperial
Majesty, the T'ang Emperor of China."

There were gasps from the assembled noblemen, and
Daimigi sucked in his breath through his teeth. "This
cannot be allowed, Your Majesty! Foreign emissaries have
been banned from the Imperial Palace!"

Netsubo turned and bowed to Daimigi. "If it please
Your Excellency, there is no emissary. There is only the
gift."

The Emperor gave a little chuckle. "Rather like a certain book I saw some months ago, eh Daimigi-san?" His
remark was rewarded with a dubious sidelong glare from
the Chancellor.

"Bring in this gift, Netsubo-san," commanded the Emperor. "For if there is no official emissary, no one need
think that we have 'officially' accepted it." Netsubo bowed
and left the room. In a few moments, he returned, followed by four strong men. They bore on their shoulders
a platform on which sat an enormous red lacquer box,
whose sides were decorated with gold and black inlaid
dragons. Great knots of black silk cord were at each of
the corners of the box, and as the men set the platform
down, they began to untie these. All at once, the four
sides and top of the box fell away, revealing what appeared to be a loose pile of black, red and gold cloth.
Then the cloth began to shift, and a veiled figure slowly

sat up. The porters removed this veil to reveal the most beautiful woman the Emperor had ever seen.

Her face was as pale and smooth as the finest porcelain. Her mouth was round and tiny, wtih lips the color of red plum blossoms. Her dark eyes shone through elegant, narrow lids. Golden pins and combs held her thick, lustrous black hair in an elaborate coif. She was swathed in a Chinese court robe of red, covered with embroidered black and gold dragons. In her lap, two tiny, delicate hands held a silver flute. Everything about her seemed so perfect, the Emperor could scarcely believe she was real.

"The Emperor of China," Netsubo said, "has heard that Our Beloved Majesty has a taste for beautiful flautists."

"What is your name?" the Emperor asked her.

"If it please Your Majesty, this insignificant one is called Su K'an." Her voice was high and soft and sweet.

"This is most . . . irregular," Daimigi murmured, looking at the woman with concern. The Emperor was pleased to see that even the Chancellor seemed taken with her beauty.

"Perhaps we should ask her to play something," suggested one of the noblemen, "and see if she is as good as our Uguisu."

The Emperor nodded and waved his fan at Su K'an, "Play something for us."

Su K'an smiled and raised the silver flute. The tune she played was light and cheerful, the notes bright like sparkling water, and equally dazzling. The Emperor felt his spirits buoyed, his cares melting like morning mist. He was reminded of times long ago, early spring or autumn mornings when he would stare at the sky and think of nothing at all.

But soon the tune ended, leaving the Emperor feeling refreshed but dissatisfied. "Play us another!" he asked.

"If it please Your Great Majesty, that is the only tune I can play, although I can add variations."

"Oh. Well, do so, then."

She obeyed, and the Emperor felt exactly the same throughout the song, and exactly the same when it ended. He was about to request that she play once more when he saw the cat Hinata enter the room. "Ah, My Lady Hinata! What do you think of our new flautist?"

The yellow cat stopped well away from Su K'an, raised her nose and cautiously sniffed the air. Slowly, Hinata's ears flattened against her head and she lowered herself into a crouch. A low growl rumbled in her throat as her fur began to stand on end.

"Hinata?" the Emperor said, confused.

Suddenly, the cat sprang at the Chinese woman, howling and spitting and slashing with her claws. The Emperor stood and rushed to her, grabbing the cat below her forelegs and raising her up. "Hinata! What are you doing? Have you gone mad?" The Emperor shook the cat for emphasis.

Hinata hissed at the Emperor.

"How dare you!" The Emperor flung the cat towards a far wall where she fell heavily on her side. "Guard!" called the Emperor, and two Inner Guardsmen came rushing in. "Chase the cat Hinata out of the Palace grounds. She is banished! And should she try to return . . . kill her."

The guardsmen bowed and went to do their duty, but Hinata had already slipped out through the shoji and disappeared. With a sigh, the Emperor turned to Su K'an who was taking her hands from her face. He was pleased to note no sharp claw had marred its perfection. "Are you all right?"

"Yes, Your Gracious Majesty. The cat did not harm me."

The Emperor sat back on his dais with a fleeting smile of relief and embarrassment. "I regret that you were subjected to such a disturbance. She has never acted like that before."

"Perhaps it is because I smell . . . foreign."

"Yes, perhaps. Well, you needn't worry about her any longer. Please play your delightful tune once more."

With a pleased smile, the courtesan again raised the silver flute to her lips.

Moon Viewing

Water lapped quietly against the side of the dragon-boat on the lake in the Seriyō Garden. The autumn evening was cool, but the air still held some of the scent and warmth of late summer. Somewhere, away on the lake's edge, crickets sang a lively tune while fireflies danced. Overhead, the full moon shone brilliant, so bright it hurt to look at it. But, then, this was the Fifteenth Day of the Eighth Month, when the moon was said to be at its most beautiful. The Moon God had not disappointed the mortals below this year, and all at court sat out on balconies, or on boats in the lakes of the palace gardens, to admire.

Fujiwara no Daimigi scarcely allowed any of this to distract him as he carefully watched the other two people in the imperial dragon boat. The Emperor and the Chinese courtesan Su K'an sat laughing together, seemingly oblivious to Daimigi's gaze, though at times Su K'an would glance in his direction.

She is an interesting mystery, thought Daimigi. Unlike the other ladies at court, she never hid behind a kicho, but boldly displayed her beauty before all. And her beauty was such that no one objected. Tonight, Daimigi noticed, her face seemed as pale and radiant as the moon. Many noble courtiers had risked imperial ire by openly writing poems to her playing upon the comparison. But the Emperor was so enchanted with her that he didn't seem to mind.

But where did she come from? Daimigi had made some discreet inquiries and learned that no one knew of any expeditions to arrive from China bearing such a "gift." The scholars he had spoken to knew of no such thing, although they also said their Emperor acted in mysterious ways, and certainly would not have informed such lowly ones as they of his intentions. None of Netsubo's household knew, or was willing to say, how he learned of her. Were it not for her beauty, and refined manners that were clearly the product of a life in an imperial court, Daimigi would be highly suspicious.

And what does our Emperor intend to do with her? I can only hope she does not distract him from his duty. The one good thing about her arrival, Daimigi considered, was that the upstart Uguisu was now further from the Emperor's mind. In the distance, an occasional mournful strain of her flute music would drift out over the water. *Drifting away she is indeed. With luck, the Emperor will send her away soon. Particularly if "luck" is given some assistance. Ah, well.* Daimigi sighed and shifted his weight, causing the boat to rock a little. *Let us see how the coins fall for me this evening.*

"My lord," Daimigi said to the Emperor, "perhaps on this suitably romantic evening we should at last discuss that matter that was brought up at the sumo selection—your marriage to my daughter."

The Emperor turned and in the dim light the Chancellor could see he was scowling fiercely. "No, I do not see that it is appropriate to bring up that matter at this time.

How could you suggest such a thing with Su K'an as my guest here?"

Because I am informing her of her place, you dolt.

But before Daimigi could reply with something considerably more polite, Su K'an laughed and said, "Oh, do not worry about me. Your Lord Chancellor is right."

The Emperor looked at her in astonishment. "What?"

"It is indeed proper. The ladies of your court have explained the situation to me and I understand. Your people would no more accept a foreign Empress than would mine. And I am told your Empresses always come from the Fujiwara family. So of course you should marry the Chancellor's daughter."

Amida help us! thought Daimigi, *a reasonable woman!*

"You would . . . approve?" the Emperor asked.

Su K'an laughed again. "It is not my place to give approval to Your Majesty. Besides, I am not so proud to think that I might hold the heart of an Emperor for long."

"You may hold mine, Su K'an for a very long time. And you would have no need to feel jealous. Daimigi's daughter is still a child."

"Then that will be even more charming," said Su K'an. "I would be happy to take the child into my household and treat her as my own. I could train her in the ways of my own court, and make quite a lady of her."

"One moment," said Daimigi, trying to keep the anger from his voice. "I am not certain I would approve of this 'training.' As a Fujiwara, my daughter has been given the best education in court etiquette, graces and skills. She has no need of foreign influences."

Su K'an bowed. "Forgive me, Your Excellency. I am quite sure you have given her the best training available in this tiny island Empire. But remember that I am from the ancient and mighty Empire of China. And no doubt there is a thing or two that I know that your daughter does not."

The Emperor laughed gently. "She has a point, Daimigi-san, you must admit."

Calming himself with effort, Daimigi said, "My lord, as you may recall, the reason your illustrious ancestor ceased sending embassies to China was because the T'ang dynasty was seen to be in decline and—"

"But it is clear," said the Emperor, "from the appearance of Su K'an here, that they still have much to offer us."

"It would also please me," said Su K'an, "to assist the young Empress when she has her child. For one so young will surely need an older woman to guide her. Since the only child I have had was a son I lost long ago, it would please me to help raise another."

"You are good to me, Su K'an," the Emperor said softly.

"It suits me to be good to you," she replied with a small smile, her dark eyes glittering.

"Your Majesty, I will not allow—"

"You will not allow what, Daimigi-san?" asked the Emperor. "You are not in a position to not allow things. In fact, I will only marry your daughter if she is given over to the care of Su K'an. And her child as well. Now what say you?"

Daimigi let out his breath through clenched teeth. It was most important that a Fujiwara become Empress, and he could only hope her Fujiwara training would not become tainted by this foreign influence. As for the son and heir, well, there would be time enough to gain control of him. "Very well, Your Majesty. As you wish."

The Emperor sighed. "Well, now that is settled. You may pick whatever day you wish for the wedding feast."

"But it should be soon," said Su K'an. "For the sake of your people."

"If you think so," said the Emperor. "Soon, then." He returned to his sake cup and the beauty of Su K'an's face.

Daimigi roughly leaned back against the boat cushions and frowned. He had his way, but it seemed more of a defeat than a victory. As he tried to let his spirits settle, he saw Su K'an lean over the water as she laughed at the Emperor's clever words. As she did so, Daimigi thought there was something odd about her reflection in the water. But before he could sit up further to look, she reached her hand down to rinse out a cup, disturbing the reflection.

Hmm. An illusion of the moonlight, and my anger, no doubt. Nothing more.

The Competition

"Must I be in the same room with her?" Uguisu asked. She sat near the veranda blinds, gazing out at the falling leaves that were heavy with autumn raindrops.

"Of course you must," said Nikao. "It is part of the form of the uta-awase. The subjects of a poetry contest must be present to lend inspiration. But we must find something more colorful for you to wear, so that you will not seem so . . .drab next to her."

"It will be so much fun," said Kitsune. "We haven't had a good competition in the Palace for too long. Especially one of such importance."

"Importance?" asked Shonasaki.

"Yes, importance, little Head-in-the-Clouds. The Chancellor himself organized the contest, and he and the Emperor will both be judges."

Shonasaki gave Kitsune a long, measuring stare.

Uguisu felt only heaviness in her chest. "So today my lord Emperor chooses between her and me." She knew Su K'an was attracting a growing portion of the court's attention. Courtiers and servants went about humming her one song, and expressed more interest in Chinese literature and culture. Uguisu was mostly ignored. In one way she was grateful for this; the Emperor no longer came to her, so she could no longer endanger him. But she found that she missed his kind attention. And it saddened her that he had not even replied to her warning poem.

"Nonsense!" said Kitsune. "They will be choosing the best poetry, not the best person."

"At Court," murmured Shonasaki, "that is much the same thing."

The day continued to be dreary and rainy, and the Court was happy for an event that encouraged them to remain indoors. The audience chamber of the Seriyō Den was quite full of perfumed ladies and noblemen—which made Uguisu feel all the more shy and nervous.

Because Su K'an did not use a kicho, Uguisu was denied one, and had to sit openly before the assembled nobles. How they stared! She felt absolutely naked, despite her twelve kimonos and court cloak, and often hid her face behind her fan. She wondered how far she must have fallen from the Emperor's favor that he forced her to endure this.

But the noblemen stared most at Su K'an, who looked regal and magnificent in a cloak of midnight blue, patterned with chrysanthemums in gold thread. Her hair and face were perfection itself. Uguisu felt quite plain beside her, despite the bright red kimonos Nikao had found for

Uguisu to wear. Even the Emperor, sitting with the Chancellor on the Imperial dias, looked most often in Su K'an's direction.

If only once more he would look upon me fondly.

Uguisu sighed and noticed that Su K'an was smiling at her. It was not a pleasant smile. Uguisu somehow managed to smile in return and bowed. Su K'an merely nodded. Something about the Chinese woman's eyes seemed familiar, the way they gleamed like dark burning coals. But Uguisu could not remember where she had seen such eyes before.

Maid-servants entered with bowls of rice and bottles of sake for refreshment. "Let us have some music as we dine!" called out one of the noblemen. "Yes!" called another. "Now that we have both flautists together, let them play a duet."

There were immediate murmurs of agreement throughout the hall, and the Emperor waved his fan to order it done. Uguisu trembled with fear and wondered if she could possibly protest. She had never played a duet with anyone. And she felt intimidated by the very presence of Su K'an.

The courtesan leaned towards her and said softly, "You needn't worry. I play only one tune. It should be easy enough for you to follow."

Then Su K'an began, playing on her silvery flute the cheery, bright song she always played. And Uguisu raised her wooden flute and tried to play along. But where Su K'an's notes were merriest, Uguisu's were sad, for her feelings of fear and isolation kept creeping into her music. The discord this created was horrible to hear, and after only a minute Uguisu had to stop. "This is impossible," she said. "Forgive this inadequate one, my lords, but my hands play according to my moods, not my will. I cannot follow another."

"A great pity," said the Emperor. "I had hoped there could be harmony between the two of you."

The double meaning was not lost on Uguisu. She closed her eyes and sighed again. "But let Su K'an continue!" said one of the nobles. "Even if Uguisu cannot play, let us still hear that happy tune."

So Su K'an began again the same song she always played, that the court never seemed to tire of.

Uguisu, meanwhile, hid her face behind her sleeves, wanting to melt into the floor out of embarassment and shame.

When Su K'an finished, the Emperor signaled that it was time for the poetry contest to begin. The dishes and bottles were taken away and a space was cleared in the center of the room, crowding the nobles against the kichos of their ladies. Then Shonasaki, Nikao and Kitsune came forward, and sat in a line to the left of the Emperor. They were to be the Team of the Left, and would write poems in favor of Uguisu. Page boys placed paper, brushes and inkstones before each of the ladies-in-waiting. Nikao seemed to have difficulty controlling her giggles, and Uguisu worried about what poems she might write. The Team of the Right, consisting of three of Su K'an's ladies-in-waiting, seated themselves at the Emperor's right and were also provided with writing implements. Uguisu knew almost nothing about them, save that they had some scholarship in Chinese literature, and they were highly regarded at court. No doubt it was thought that this would aid them in their poetic defense of Su K'an.

Next, the gentlemen who would read the poems aloud were announced and came forward. Kazenatsu would read for the Team of the Left. Uguisu wondered if this showed some favor for her side from the Fujiwara—for it would be ironic if true. But after a moment, seeing the looks Kazenatsu and Kitsune exchanged, she realized it was a favor for someone else.

Then the reader was announced for the Team of the Right—the Minister of the Household, Echizen no Netsubo.

Uguisu felt as if struck by lightning. *My own father reads for the team against me!* She searched his face for some reassurance, some indication that he felt it was only a game. But her father would not even look at her.

The Emperor slapped his fan against the dais to silence the murmuring crowd. "Let the uta-awase begin! It has been decided that the Team of the Left shall be first."

Shonasaki bent over her paper and began to write. It had been said the night before that having Shonasaki first writer of the team would give Uguisu a good strong beginning—for the first writer invented the imagery that all the other poets would have to ring changes upon. But Uguisu felt it hardly mattered now.

The poem was handed to Kazenatsu, who read in a strong, clear voice,

> "Deep as the waters of Lake Biwa,
> is the music of our lady,
> upon whom Benten smiles."

There came murmurs of approval at this poem, and even Uguisu was amazed by Shonasaki's skill. Benten was the only goddess among the seven deities of luck, and was the patron of music and literature, as well as the Bringer of Happiness. She was also associated with wealth and happy marriage, and was said to live with the Dragon King beneath the waters of Lake Biwa. Not only was Uguisu smiled upon by Benten, but the poem strongly identified her with the goddess. A powerful image indeed.

The first writer for the Team of the Right, however, quickly finished her poem and handed it to Netsubo, who read,

> "Sunlight on the waters of Lake Biwa,
> Is the music of our lady,
> Who has also known the court of Dragons."

Expressions of approval were made to this poem also, whose last line led to many interesting interpretations.

It now became Nikao's turn, and Uguisu worried as she hesitated, it seemed, too long. But in a few minutes, Nikao managed to set brush to paper and shortly handed a poem to Kazenatsu.

> "Sunlight comes and goes with clouds and nightfall,
> Yet beneath the Heavens Biwa remains,
> Deep and constant."

Uguisu was not happy with this poem. Not only did it simplify the poetic imagery, but it brought in hints of her relations to the Emperor. Was Nikao saying Su K'an was a passing fancy while Uguisu would remain? Was she suggesting Su K'an's affections for the Emperor were shallow? There were disapproving mutterings from the nobles as the second of the Team of the Right began her poem. When Netsubo read it, Uguisu realized just how foolish Nikao's poem had been.

> "The waters of Lake Biwa are nourished
> By the rains of Heaven,
> Only to flow away, out to the sea."

It was a very subtle rebuke, subtly handled. It implied Uguisu did not return the care of the Emperor, preferring to put her energies into her own interests. Uguisu closed her eyes, praying that Kitsune could somehow salvage the situation. Kitsune was not as poetically inclined as Shonasaki, but she could be clever, when she chose. With some relief, Uguisu saw her write her poem very quickly. Kazenatsu read,

> "Without the sea, there are no rains from Heaven,
> Biwa is more than Heaven's mirror,
> Her dragons lie within her, not above."

For a moment there was stunned silence. Then came angry murmurs from the crowd. Did Uguisu think herself above the Emperor!? Uguisu saw the Emperor scowl at Kitsune and hid her face behind her sleeves, knowing she had lost. *How could Kitsune say such things?*

The last poet on the Team of the Right snatched up her brush and eagerly began to write, but with a snap of his fan the Emperor ordered her to stop. Turning to Kitsune, he asked, "What does your poem mean?"

"It is merely an expression, my lord, of my lady's view of the importance of things in the world."

"Is it so?" the Emperor stared at Uguisu. She longed to shout out "No, no, it isn't true!" but the Emperor did not give her the chance. "I have heard enough!" he growled. "This contest is over! I declare the Team of the Right, and Su K'an, the winners. They may join us in the Imperial Dining Hall for the celebration banquet." The Emperor rose, and without another look at Uguisu, strode out of the room.

Uguisu tried to stand and protest, but found herself pushed roughly to the floor. Nobles shoved past her, ignoring her cries of dismay, to surround Su K'an and her team. Uguisu felt frightened in the crush of bodies pressing on her but ignoring her. Suddenly, a woman's arm reached out and grabbed Uguisu's sleeve, pulling her close. It was Shonasaki, who managed to pull Uguisu through the seething tide of people, until they finally got outside into the garden. They collapsed wearily beneath a nearly bare cherry tree. Uguisu laid her head on Shonasaki's shoulder and wept.

"I am so sorry, my lady," said the poet. "I had no idea it would be like this. I would not have been a part of it if I had known."

"What shall I do? I have said nothing like what Kitsune said. Why did she say that?"

"I do not know," said Shonasaki, stroking Uguisu's hair.

Uguisu sobbed, gripping Shonasaki's shoulders, then suddenly realized that something was missing. "My flute! Shonasaki—where is my flute?"

"I don't know, I did not see—oh, no, My Lady! You must not go back there!"

Ignoring her, Uguisu ran back toward the building. But, careless of her footing, she tripped on a tree root just before the veranda. As she fell, sprawled on the ground, a bit of color caught her eye. Just in front of her she saw her wooden flute, lying broken and trampled among the damp autumn leaves.

Ladies Parting

"I wonder where she has gone," said Shonasaki, gazing through the bamboo curtain as the last leaves fell from the cherry trees beyond the veranda.

"She is no longer our concern," said Kitsune, who was folding and packing her kimonos and cloaks.

"How can you just sit there and say that?" said Nikao, wiping away a tear with her sleeve. "Didn't you care for Our Lady at all?"

"She was a little fool. She only has gotten what she deserved."

"But I never heard her say anything like what your poem said."

"But her actions spoke loudly enough, didn't they? It was clear she put her own concerns over those of the Emperor. Daimigi-sama merely wanted it made clear to His Majesty and the Court."

"Daimigi-sama!" said Shonasaki, snapping her head around to stare at Kitsune. "What did the Chancellor have to do with this?"

"Nothing, really. He merely suggested the tone my poem should take and—"

"Traitor!" yelled Nikao as she pushed Kitsune over and began pulling her hair. Shonasaki quickly pulled her off Kitsune and held her, but the poet glared at Kitsune.

"How dare you call me traitor, you lump of ricemush!" Kitsune said, righting herself. "It was Uguisu who was treacherous, not I! She put us in a dangerous position. I have saved us! You should be thanking me!"

"No doubt the Chancellor will be thanking you as well," Shonasaki said softly.

"As he should! I made the problem clear to Our Majesty who has now solved it. And I shall have a place in the Fujiwara household now."

"Has Kazenatsu offered to openly declare you as his wife?"

"No . . . not yet. But he will, soon enough. I don't know what you are so angry about. The Fujiwara will offer the two of you places as well, if you choose."

"I will refuse anything they offer me," said Shonasaki.

"Heh! So go become a nun and live in poverty, writing sutras until you die of hunger. And you, Nikao, you could have a place. Hidoi, they say, still seeks a wife."

"You can't be serious," said Shonasaki.

"It is her choice to make."

"I don't know," murmered Nikao. "I think I will go home."

"Fine. Go back to your family, and they can marry you off to some skinny silk merchant for whom you can have babies till you drop. Oh, you two are such fools!" Kitsune jumped to her feet and balled her fists. Shonasaki was surprised to see a tear rolling down Kitsune's cheek, leaving a rivulet in her white face powder. "I do all I can to help you and you take the side of that selfish little flute-player! Well, I hope Benten smiles upon you—you will need smiles from all seven Gods of Luck, for no one in this Palace will be of any help to you anymore!" Kitsune swiftly picked up the packed clothing-basket and hurried out of the room with a sob.

Shonasaki hugged Nikao, who was weeping. "It has all gone so wrong, somehow."

"You once said," gasped Nikao, "that all things of beauty come to an end. It is *aware*."

"Yes. But there is more happening here. It is not the normal loss of beauty in time. Too many people now actively seek its destruction. I fear for us all.

"Our fortunes tumble with the leaves of autumn,
And now, I wonder, will there come a spring?"

WINTER

The snowflakes drifting down—
Behind them earth and sky
Are crouching, silent.
                    —Hashin

WINTER STORM

LIGHTNING FLASHED IN THE night, illuminating barren trees and sword-sharp grasses in a blinding white glare. The thunder followed, rumbling over the hissing of the rain like the booming of a huge funeral drum. Uguisu staggered through the nightmare landscape, her torn, wet kimonos clinging to her arms and legs. Icy raindrops splattered on her face and hair, and ran in chilling rivulets beneath her clothes. Teeth chattering helplessly, she shuddered with the cold.

If I can just reach the river Kamo, she thought, *I will end my troubles in its waters.* But she had spent days wandering the city, eating and sleeping very little. And the chill of the storm sapped what was left of her strength. She grasped the slick branches of a dead tree, unable to move any further.

Lightning flashed again and Uguisu moaned, putting her back against the wet trunk of the tree and flinging her arms wide. "Strike me! End this miserable life with your fire! Strike me!"

But the thunder rolled on, leaving cold, wet darkness behind. Uguisu's cheeks grew tight and she felt herself starting to cry, but her face was so filled with raindrops she could not tell if tears joined them. She slid down against the tree until she knelt in the mud between its roots. *How can I be so tied to this life when I am so ready to leave? My body is like a stone weight holding me here.*

Another bolt lit up the night. Silhouetted in its flash was a large, hulking figure with wild hair and grimacing face. Uguisu caught her breath. *An Oni! A demon who has come to escort me to the gates of Hell!* Summoning all her strength, she flung herself across the path of the striding figure. "Here I am, Oni-san! If you have mercy, make my death swift and carry me from this cold world!"

"Eh? What is this?" said the figure in a deep, gruff voice. Uguisu felt strong hands grasp her arms and raise her till she stood. "Who are you?"

Uguisu wearily wondered if the demon's question was philosophical, and if her answer might determine to which of the many afterlives she might be taken. She felt quite beyond deep thought. "I am no one. I am nothing!"

The strong hands shook her. "No one is nothing!" growled the deep voice. "What is your name?"

"This . . . this lowly one was once called Uguisu."

"Uguisu? Echizen no Uguisu, the Imperial Flute-Player?"

"I am Imperial no longer. I have been banished from the Palace. And my flute is broken. And my father has disowned me, so I am Echizen no longer. Truly, I am nothing, Oni-san."

"I am not an oni! I am Kuma. And you are not nothing. Come with me."

He has the form of a man, yet he is called 'bear.' Might His Majesty or my father have sent . . . no. He must be an animal-spirit, come to take me to his forest. No mortal of this world would take an interest in me now.

She felt his strong arms lift her up and she was carried through the rain back into the city. In time they came to a small house that had clearly once been a place of some nobility and elegance, but now was falling into ruin. *How like myself,* thought Uguisu.

Kuma carried her through the wild garden and onto the veranda. There he rapped on the latticed shutters. "I have returned, Katte-san! Open up!"

The sound of running feet came from within, and the shutters were unlatched and opened. Within stood a woman who looked vaguely familiar to Uguisu.

"Ah, Kuma-san! Did you find any—Who is this?"

"This is the Lady Uguisu, Katte-san. I found her by the Kamo River."

Kuma carried Uguisu to the central room of the house, where a small floor-hearth radiated welcome warmth. As Uguisu was set down beside the hearth, she wanted to protest that she was no longer a lady and unworthy of such kindness. But the change in temperature caused her to shiver violently and she could not speak.

"Lady Uguisu!" said Katte. "The Lady of the Pine Kicho! Oh, what has happened?" Katte put her hands on Uguisu's cheeks. "You are so cold! We must get you out of those wet clothes."

Kuma looked at Uguisu with concern. Katte began to peel the wet kimonos off of Uguisu—a difficult task, since

Uguisu could not help, she shivered so. Kuma disappeared into an adjoining room, then returned with an aloeswood chest that he set beside Katte. Then with a nod, Kuma left again.

"You must tell me—oh, I see you cannot speak just now. Dear me, how your teeth chatter! Do try to hold still, please." Setting aside Uguisu's wet silk robes, Katte pulled out of the chest some clean but patched cotton kimonos and wrapped them around Uguisu's still shaking form. "Well, I shall tell you what has happened with myself, then, since we last met." Katte recounted to Uguisu the story of her promotion at court, the cruelties of the ladies and the Chancellor's present. "I gave half the gold to my family, and with the rest I went to find Kuma. Now, you see, he and I can finally marry for we are at last of the same rank—which is to say no rank at all."

Uguisu felt warmer and no longer shook as much. The cotton kimonos were soft and comforting against her chilled skin, but she noticed they were old and patched with care. "You are so kind. I am so sorry to be a burden imposed upon you."

Katte laughed. "Oh, you must not feel you are a burden. It appears to be my fate these days to be a caretaker of strays. See?" She pointed to a corner across the hearth.

Uguisu looked. There, seated among the empty rice sacks in the shadows, was the cat Hinata. She seemed thinner than she had been in the Palace, and her fur was scruffier. But she still looked at Uguisu with penetrating golden eyes.

Her gaze brought back all of Uguisu's sorrow and guilt. Leaning on Katte, Uguisu found herself spilling out her entire story—how the guardian spirit instructed her, how she obeyed by denying the Emperor, then disobeyed to save his life. She told how she was supplanted by the

Chinese lady and expelled after the poetry contest. "What terrible things must I have done in past lives, for my karma to have earned me a fate such as this?" Uguisu could not keep back tears of self-pity and she wept on Katte's shoulder.

"So that is what happened," said Katte. "But why didn't you tell someone at the Palace this? Surely you could have found someone to help and understand you."

"I tried. I tried to tell my father, to have him warn the Fujiwara Chancellor. But I fear my father did not believe me and told Daimigi-san nothing. I sent a warning poem to the Emperor. But because I did not know what eyes would see it, I had to be circumspect in my wording. Either His Majesty did not understand me, or chose to ignore me. I could not tell everything, because my mother's family is forbidden from the Palace. My father would have been punished for bringing me to Court. And I might have been executed. Though, perhaps, that would have been the best thing."

"Nonsense! It is unfair that you should be punished for doing what is right. Surely some wise kami, or the Amidabha himself will understand. You will have great karma for your next life, I am sure."

Uguisu felt something soft against her cheek and turned her face to see what it was. The cat Hinata had climbed onto her lap and was sniffing her face. Gently, Hinata began to lick the tears from Uguisu's cheek.

"You see?" said Katte. "Even Hinata-san forgives you."

Katte gave Uguisu a bowl of rice to eat. Then she led her to a sleeping mat behind a screen whose paper panels were stained and torn. Uguisu lay down, and Katte covered her with more cotton robes. "You rest now," said Katte, and she withdrew to return to the hearth.

Weariness overtook Uguisu and her arms and legs felt

heavy and cold. Her chest felt heavy as well and she found herself breathing slower.

She heard Kuma reenter the room, and he and Katte began speaking softly, though Uguisu could hear them clearly through the paper screen.

"Of course we must help her," Katte was saying, "but our funds are running low, though we have been frugal. I do not know how long—"

"You need not worry," said Kuma. "I have seen men in the Guard die from weather less severe than what she has been through. I doubt she will last another day."

Katte gasped and began to weep. "So soon? Then . . . then we must find a priest to attend her. Oh, but we cannot afford a priest!"

"I know of one priest who would serve her for no payment," said Kuma, "if I can find him."

So, I am dying, thought Uguisu. She was surprised at her own lack of fear. Feeling the coldness creeping through her, she knew Kuma was right. It would be soon.

Hearing the crackle of straw beside her, Uguisu opened her eyes and saw Hinata standing there. The cat stepped onto Uguisu's chest and lay down, tucking her paws beneath her. With the weight of the cat pressing on her, Uguisu found breathing even more difficult. *Does the cat wish to hasten my death? As punishment or mercy, I wonder.*

Hinata began to purr and a curious but delicious warmth spread out from beneath her, filling Uguisu's body and driving the cold from her limbs. She felt a peaceful darkness overtake her. *If this is to be my death*, thought Uguisu, *it is better than I deserve.*

The Silver Mirror

"The rain has turned to snow," said Su K'an as she sat looking out through the bamboo blinds. "Raiden, the Thunder Demon, has spent his anger and Tsukiyomi, the Moon Goddess, now appears from behind the clouds. It is an auspicious sign for your wedding, My Lord."

The Emperor laughed gently as he gazed on her, still entranced by her beauty. "Is divination another one of your many talents, Su K'an? I am surprised and pleased that you know so much about our gods. Though I am not sure that the appearance of the Kami of the Realm of Darkness could be called 'auspicious.'"

Su K'an smiled. "But of course she is. The 'Realm of Darkness' is night, is it not? Do you not wish to have many pleasant nights after your wedding?"

"I have had many pleasant nights already," said the Emperor. "And it is Kwannon, Goddess of Mercy, who has smiled on me by bringing you into my life."

Su K'an looked down demurely, but no trace of a blush stained her perfect pale features. "My Lord is most kind, but it is not me you should be thinking of right now. You still have two nights to spend with your little bride-to-be. Then you will have your grand wedding banquet and I may take joy in seeing you with your new little Empress beside you."

The Emperor laughed again and shook his head. "You are amazing, Su K'an. I know of no other woman who would be pleased to see her lover married to someone else."

"But as I have explained, my lord, I shall be gaining a family. And that shall do more to fulfill my dreams than you can know. Is that not cause for joy?"

The Emperor sighed, again thanking his guardian star

for sending him such a good-natured lady. "Very well. I shall find my duty more pleasant for knowing it brings you joy." It would be nearly the only pleasure, the Emperor reflected, for Daimigi's daughter was as shy and uncomfortable as Uguisu—but the child did not have the temerity, or the option, to say no. "But before I leave to undertake this night's duties, I have a gift for you, Su K'an."

"A gift? My lord is too generous to this lowly one."

"Nonsense. The gift is hardly worthy of such a beauty as you. Yet I wish you to have it as a small token of the great affection I have for you. Now, please close your eyes a moment. I want this to be a surprise."

Su K'an laughed and turned her face away, eyes shut. The Emperor smiled to himself and went to a beautifully inlaid sandalwood box. Lifting off the lid, he pulled out a bundle of white silk. He carefully unwrapped the silk to reveal a magnificent silver mirror. Its back was decorated with an image of Benten in her aspect as Goddess of Beauty, and studded with pearls and mother-of-pearl and emeralds. The craftsman who made the mirror claimed it had been ceremonially purified in the waters of Lake Biwa. It was said this blessed the mirror with the power to show the true, inner beauty of whoever was reflected on its surface.

The Emperor wondered if Su K'an's beauty could be enhanced in any way. Out of curiosity, he approached her from behind, holding out the mirror. He hoped to catch a glimpse of her reflection in the mirror while she sat unaware. But as he held the mirror near her face, he saw Su K'an's lustrous raven hair reflected as a frazzled grey mass. And the image of her face was ashen and wrinkled, as if centuries old. "What is this?" exclaimed the Emperor. Something was terribly wrong.

"My Lord?" said Su K'an, turning. Her gaze fell upon the mirror and her eyes widened. In the reflection, a red glow lit within her eyes and her lips pulled back in a snarl. Lashing out with one arm, she smashed the mirror out of the Emperor's hand. With an unpleasant, embarrassed laugh, she said, "Forgive me, Your Majesty, but I dislike mirrors. They make me seem vain and—"

"No," breathed the Emperor. "I can scarcely believe it, but it is too late. I have seen." The Emperor moved slowly away from her. "You are an oni! A demon!"

"Not quite, my foolish, impetuous Lord."

The Emperor watched frozen in horror as the beautiful form of Su K'an melted and collapsed in upon herself. The perfect face shriveled like a pale rotting fruit. Her scarlet robes slowly settled, steaming and charred, to the floor. A grey column rose above the foul remains and resolved into the ancient, wizened form the Emperor had seen in the mirror.

"I am a distant relative, though not a direct ancestor of yours. My family had been treated most unfairly by the Fujiwara. Had you simply accepted me, my vengeance against them would have been gradual and assured. You might have lived more happy years in ignorance. Your little bride would bear you a son, in whom I would incorporate the soul of my own son. He would have become a great wizard-emperor, who could have vanquished the Fujiwara forever. But now," she said, pointing a gnarled, spectral hand at the Emperor, "you have ruined any chance you had at being part of our grand design. Our vengeance will continue—that is all that remains to us. But we must see that you can no longer interfere."

The ghost rushed at the Emperor and he felt sharp coldness fill his muscles and bones. He tried to crawl to the shoji to call for a guard, but with all his effort he could only fall upon his side.

"It is useless," the spirit whispered in his head. "Now you are mine."

Frigid pain shot through the Emperor and he cried out in a long, silent scream.

Snow and Ashes

Dark, ash-laden smoke rose high in a column from the funeral pyre, mingling with flurries of light falling snow. Buddhist priests surrounding the bier chanted the Nirvana Sutra, while Shinto priests shook their wands of purification.

Takenoko felt no sorrow as he watched the substance that had been his father burn and ascend the ladder of smoke to Heaven. His only regret was that he remained behind, still tied to this world. The chanting of the priests reminded him of an old poem he had learned as a child for a writing exercise:

> "Springtime blossoms bright
>   with life
> Someday scatter on the wind
> Who among us lives beyond
>   his time?
> Now that my soul has become a pilgrim
> Dreams no longer trouble me
> And fleeting pleasures cloud my mind
>   no more."

Fate has taken from me all I have cared for. Uguisu is gone. My father is dead. Why should my heart still be concerned with worldly things?

As Takenoko continued to stare at the ascending smoke, watching the ashes dancing with the snowflakes, he felt a tightness begin to ease within him. His heart felt light, as if he, too, were a mote dancing on the wind. A rush of exhilaration coursed through him. *Have I, at last, set my foot upon the path to Heaven?* Hours later, the question still occupied Takenoko's mind as he came down the path from the burial ground. The path was lined with stone statues of gods and demons, bodhisattvas and other seated figures, wearing hats and epaulets of fresh-fallen snow. Takenoko passed these without a glance. So absorbed was he with his thoughts that he scarcely noticed when one figure stood and spoke to him.

"Takenoko-san."

"What? Oh. Kuma-san. Where did you come from?"

"I have been waiting for you to finish your services. I have something to ask you."

"Very well. But I was not conducting services, I was attending. It was my father's funeral."

"Oh." Kuma's shoulders slumped and his face drooped sadly. "I am so very sorry, Takenoko."

He did not know my father well. Why does he mourn? "Do not weep for him, Kuma-san. He is now free of the cares of this world, unlike you and I. Our souls deserve more pity and sorrow than his."

"Indeed. You are right, Takenoko."

"Now what was it you wished to ask?"

"What? Oh. No, I cannot ask it of you now. Not with your father—never mind." Kuma turned and began to walk away.

"Wait, Kuma-san!" Takenoko caught up to Kuma. "Did I not say that I do not mourn him? Ask me whatever you wish."

Kuma continued walking. "It was . . . just a small service Katte and I wished you to perform. It is nothing."

"A service? Ah! A wedding? I would be pleased to—"

"No, not a wedding."

"What, then?"

"No. It would be too sad to ask it of you."

"A funeral?"

"A deathwatch. Perhaps, by now, a funeral. But I shall find another priest."

"I will perform this service for you, Kuma. Helping others to be free of this world may help me on my own Path to Heaven. Now tell me what sort of person I will be attending, so I may choose an appropriate sutra. Is he a nobleman?"

"She was once a noble . . ."

"A woman, then." Suddenly Takenoko's stomach went cold. "Do I know this woman?"

"She is . . . a friend of Katte's."

"But do I know her?" Takenoko demanded. "Is it Uguisu?"

"I . . . she . . . yes."

"Then let's not waste a moment longer!"

All remnants of his former euphoria vanished as Takenoko and Kuma ran through the snowy streets of Heian Kyo. When they came to the dilapidated house, Kuma rushed up onto the veranda and pounded on the shutters.

"Katte! I have brought the priest! Open up!"

Presently, Katte's laughing voice could be heard, and she opened up the shutters smiling. "You have brought a priest? How wonderful! He can give thanks to Kwannon for us."

"Thanks?" Kuma said, confused.

"Where is she?" said Takenoko, rushing past Katte into the house.

"An impetuous priest!" Katte laughed.

"Katte, this is no time for jokes. Do you not recognize Takenoko-san? He wishes to see Uguisu right away."

"Oh, of course! She is this way." Still smiling, Katte led the two men into the central room. "You may thank whatever kami watch over us for the miracle that has happened. For there she is, and she is well!"

Seated by the hearth was Uguisu, looking pale and thin but still lovely, stroking a golden-haired cat.

Takenoko kneeled across the hearth from her, unable to speak. His heart seemed to pound like wedding drums just to be seeing her again. He had the very un-priestly desire to throw his arms around her and hold her close.

After a moment, Uguisu laughed behind her hand. "Takenoko? Is that you? You look so strange without your hair."

Her remark filled Takenoko with a sudden, keen disappointment. *Is that all she can think of to say when we have been so long apart?* Then he chided himself. *What did I expect? Why should a gardener's son mean much to her now, when she has been the consort of the Emperor himself!* He managed an awkward smile and looked at the floor. "Uguisu. I am glad to see you well. For once I am pleased to feel useless."

"Useless? Ah, because you will not chant my soul away. Has it been only a year, Takenoko-chan? It seems a lifetime has passed since I last saw you beneath the autumn leaves and told you my father's wishes."

"Indeed," said Takenoko. "It is because both our lives have changed so.

I wander lost and seek a Path to Heaven,
But my thoughts' wanderings led me near to you."

More than you know, Takenoko added to himself.

Uguisu sighed and responded,

"Though my path took me to the clouds of Heaven,
Now it is I who wander lost and aimless.

But you are not useless, Takenoko. Now that you are a
priest, you can teach me the sutras."

"Teach you?"

"I have no family now, Takenoko-chan. I have been
disowned. There is no life for me now, it seems, except to
become a nun."

Takenoko imagined what Uguisu would look like with
hair chopped short and dressed in the drab kimonos of
a nun and he felt sad. "Please reconsider, Uguisu-chan.
The Path to Heaven is not smooth, and you are so young.
It is considered ill-advised for a young girl to take vows so
early. There are too many chances for temptation in life,
and the likelihood is great that she may shame herself."

"But what other choice have I, Takenoko-chan? No
one, not even Hidoi, would marry me as I am. Perhaps I
should have followed my father's wishes and married
Hidoi after all ... it would have prevented so much
trouble. And I am too shy to enter the willow world.
What can I do?"

Takenoko caught his breath, trying to control his feelings. *I would ask to wed you, were I not a monk.* For a
moment, the dizzying possibility of renouncing his vows
to wed Uguisu tantalized him. Then he felt shame for
even considering it. Takenoko remembered the lightness
he had felt at the funeral and wondered, *Am I so easily
tempted to turn away from my Path, even now that I have placed
one foot upon it? And how can I be so callous to Uguisu's wish
to trod that same Path?* "Very well, Uguisu-chan, I shall

teach you some sutras. But do not be hasty to don a nun's robes. We shall wait and see if they suit you first."

"Thank you, Takenoko-chan." Uguisu bowed solemnly. "And perhaps when we have both left this world, we will sit on separate petals of the same lotus blossom and enjoy Heavenly peace together." She smiled.

Despite his inner turmoil, Takenoko could not help but smile in return.

Mist and Moonlight

Hidoi awoke to the incongruous scent of cherry blossoms. It was still the deep of night and all was dark around him, except for one shaft of moonlight that came through a chink in the blinds. Standing radiant in the moonlight was the most beautiful woman Hidoi had ever seen. She wore robes of purest, diaphanous white. Her skin was pale and translucent as mist. Her hair was a river of blue-black iridescence that flowed all the way to the floor.

"Well, what have we here?" Hidoi said breathlessly. "Come to see how a Fujiwara sleeps? I'll let you have a closer look."

The woman said nothing, but hid the lower half of her face coyly behind her sleeve.

Hidoi sat up and tried to catch hold of her kimono. The woman moved back, just out of reach. Yet something in her eyes indicated she was not unwilling to be caught.

Hidoi moved toward her on his knees. "Please, don't feel you have to keep up appearances here. No one is watching. I assure you, I will be most discreet."

The woman stepped gracefully back again. Then, lowering her sleeve a little, she smiled. Hidoi thought her the most charming creature on earth. He knew at once he must have her. "Do not be so aloof," he said. "It was no doubt some powerful force that brought you to me—perhaps we were once close in a previous life. You cannot ignore such karma, surely."

The woman opened her mouth in silent laughter. She moved to the blinds and pulled them aside. Looking at Hidoi, she pointed out to the veranda and the garden beyond.

Dismayed, Hidoi said, "It's rather too cold a night to sit outside, don't you think?"

The woman's eyes flashed playfully and she slipped out through the blinds.

"Wait! Don't go!" Hidoi awkwardly put on a robe and stumbled through the blinds after her. Outside, Hidoi saw her standing among the snowdrifts in the garden. Feeling chilled and slightly foolish, Hidoi hoisted himself over the veranda to join her. But as before, just as she was within reach, the woman would glide away. Hidoi soon found himself chasing her across the Palace compound. From the way she danced and floated across the snowdrifts, Hidoi realized the woman could be no creature of this world.

He had heard ancient tales of spirits who were attracted to mortal men. It was often said their charms far surpassed those of ordinary women, and, if pleased, they would often reward their earthly lovers with great wealth or happiness. Hidoi was determined not to let her get away.

But now she began to dance away faster, and Hidoi had to run as fast as he could just to keep up. He scarcely noticed when he passed through the Eastern Gate, ignoring the perplexed waves and shouts of the guards. Ever eastward, the woman led him, her movements enticing, entrancing. Through snow-blanketed alleys they ran, past dark, shuttered houses and ghostly street lanterns.

At last, as Hidoi felt his lungs about to burst from exertion, she slowed. His vision blurred by the mist of his breath, Hidoi dimly saw the woman down a slope from him, surrounded by a nimbus of reflected moonlight. From somewhere nearby came the sound of running water. Wheezing, Hidoi stumbled down the hillside. This time, as he drew near, the woman did not move away. Instead, her arms grasped his. She stepped back, drawing him with her. Her touch was cool, but Hidoi did not mind. His ardor kept him warm enough. Her face filled his vision and his only thought was her beauty.

Coldness surrounded his feet and gradually crept up his legs. Hidoi ignored this, pulling the pale woman closer to him. By the time she was completely in his arms, the coldness had spread up to his chest. But his excitement at holding her banished all fear.

The woman sighed and smiled, laying her head against his shoulder. Hidoi bent down to whisper a love poem to her. But as he opened his mouth, his nose and throat filled with ice cold water, and he felt heavy pressure on his back. *How odd,* Hidoi thought, annoyed. *Why can't I breathe?*

Scarlet Mantle

A maid had opened the blinds that separated the veranda and the main room, allowing Daimigi to look out onto the glistening snow in the garden. But the bright winter scene did not cheer Daimigi. He felt the weight of his responsibilities lying heavily upon him.

There came a light rapping on the shoji behind him, and Daimigi turned his head. "Yes?"

"It is me, father."

"Ah. Korimizu. Enter."

As the boy entered, bowed and kneeled, Daimigi marveled at how Korimizu seemed to have grown even more self-assured and composed. *One would even be tempted to wonder if behind that calm face you mourn the death of your brother. The months you have spent as General of the Palace Guards seem to have served you well.* "Tell me, Korimizu, have any of your men found that foreign woman yet?"

"No, father. There is no sign of Su K'an."

"Hmm. You have not let on why we seek her?"

"No, father. But . . ."

"But?"

"There are rumors, father."

"Rumors are unavoidable, Korimizu. You must see that they are discouraged whenever possible."

"I will try, father. But people have been disturbed by Hidoi's strange drowning. And they wonder why they have not seen His Majesty in days."

"We must continue to tell them the Emperor is resting, or observing abstinence," Daimigi said softly. "His servants have been given leave and replaced by those of our household. And the palace priests have been sent back to their temples to make preparations for his somewhat postponed wedding. Our family priest watches his Majesty now, and will divulge his condition to no one but me."

"But why must we keep his illness a secret?"

Daimigi sighed. It was, he decided, time that his son knew more of the world. "You are aware, of course, that many of the great families envy our position at court, and would like to undermine us in any way they could. But they are not the only danger. Our own family is not quite the unified pillar it seems to be. The Fujiwara are more like a great tree, with many branches. And although our line may now be the highest branch, with only a little trimming another branch could just as easily come out on top, so to speak. Do you understand what I am saying?"

"Yes, father."

"There have been suggestions that I consider resigning in favor of another who might better deal with His Majesty's . . . eccentricity. The marriage would have quelled such talk. Curse that foreign whore, her timing was perfect! Almost as if she intended to—Forgive me, Korimizu. You should not hear such things."

Daimigi saw his son shift uncomfortably, frowning with concern. Softly Korimizu said, "Some people think she might have poisoned him. Since Hidoi's death, some people are saying there are evil spirits in the Palace, and that the Emperor has been possessed."

"Some people think all illness is caused by evil spirits."

"But if they are right, shouldn't His Majesty have an exorcism?"

Daimigi scowled. "Think, Korimizu! Have you no idea how people would react to the news that their beloved Emperor, living symbol of the Empire and descendant of the Great Kami, has been possessed by a spirit? It would tear the Court apart! And where do you think the blame would fall? I would be stripped of my office for allowing this to happen to His Majesty. Our entire clan would be shamed! No, Korimizu, there can be no exorcism. Our priest will treat His Majesty with herbs and quiet rest. And we must dissemble until he recovers."

"But . . . but if His Majesty does not recover—"

"Then we must hope he lingers long enough for us to re-establish our position another way. As I told Kazenatsu the other night, I have secretly sent for the Emperor's Minamoto nephew. If the lad is agreeable enough, we might arrange for him to marry your sister. In this way we can retain our position in court."

Daimigi then noticed Korimizu's eyes had narrowed and pinched in an expresssion the Chancellor had never seen on his son's face before. "I have been taught that to serve the Emperor is our greatest honor and responsibility."

"Yes, but it is time you learned which lessons will serve you in reality. You also owe duty to your family. Remember the Sutra of Filial Piety." *He must grow up so quickly, now.* "This will be a difficult time for all of us, my son. The yearly promotions draw near. With the Emperor in mysterious circumstances, all the intrigue that hides beneath surface courtesies will rise like koi carp hungry for feeding. If the Emperor dies with the succession undecided, the strife may become destructive, even deadly. Enemies might come from anywhere, not only rival clans but our own. Do you understand?"

"Yes, father." Korimizu was staring at the mat just before him, his hands twisting in his lap.

Have I so frightened the cool Korimizu? "I am sorry, my son. Perhaps things will not go so poorly. Why don't you go practice your music or poetry? Let beauty drive away your cares for now."

But Korimizu did not move. "Father, I . . ."

"There is something else?"

"Yes, father. I must tell you something."

"Something concerning what I have said?"

Korimizu nodded, but did not meet his eyes.

"Speak, then."

In a hoarse whisper, Korimizu said, "Very early this morning, Kazenatsu came to me with a request. He wanted me to select a trustworty guard to bear a secret message and package."

"To a lover, I suppose? He really ought to be more discreet."

"No, father! He asked that the guard be brave of heart ... willing to carry a message to the warrior priests of Mount Hiei."

"Mount Hiei?"

"Yes. I told him I would arrange it. But then I grew curious. After he departed, I read the letter."

"And?"

"I think you should see it." His small hands trembling, Korimizu drew from the sleeve of his voluminous green robe a folded piece of paper which he handed to Daimigi.

The Chancellor opened it and felt his stomach grow cold with shock. The message read:

Greetings in the name of the Fujiwara to the most holy Tendai masters of Mount Hiei. We have knowledge of a certain Minamoto who has spoken contemptuously of the Almighty Buddha and the magnificent temples of your holy mountain. In five days, that person will be passing on the road below Hieizan. He will be en route to the capital to take a position of great influence in the government. We understand this pass can often be dangerous, haunted by thieves and violent men. His safe arrival is hoped for, of course, but who knows what one's karma shall lead to? May Buddha smile on your endeavors.

It was not signed, but bore the seal of the Ministry of the Right, and the crest of the Fujiwara.

"The package with it," Korimizu said softly, "contained ten bars of gold."

Daimigi tried to hold back a tsunami of anger. He tried to convince himself that Kazenatsu might only have been an unwitting messenger for the true conspirators. But the letter was in Kazenatsu's handwriting. And the seal could not have been used without the knowledge of the First Minister of the Right.

"Do you know, Korimizu, if anyone might have coerced Kazenatsu into writing this letter?"

"No, father. But, then, he and I speak little these days. When I am not at my duties, I am at my studies. His work and mine do not overlap, and he is often at . . . social gatherings."

"Yes, yes, well, can you think of anyone who might know, one we could trust to be discreet?"

"No, father. For the reasons I have said."

Daimigi sighed. He did not wish to take action without proof. "The fool. Whoever conceived this is a great fool! What if the Oe or Taira had discovered this message? What if this little plot succeeded and our family was blamed for the nephew's death? It is completely thoughtless!"

"Yes, father."

"Where is your brother now?"

"He is at the Kamo Shrine, offering prayers for a bountiful rice harvest."

Conveniently distant. But who could tell me more of his thoughts and involvement? Someone who would not expect to betray him by speaking of him. "Where is the Lady Kitsune?"

"I presume in mother's quarters."

"Find her. Send her to me, but do not reveal the reason. Make it seem like a casual request. I do not want her alarmed."

"As you wish, father." Korimizu stood to leave.

"And I'm sure you need not be told that none of what we have spoken is to be repeated."

"Of course, father." The boy hesitated.

"Yes?"

"What will you do to Kazenatsu?"

"We will see."

"And His Majesty?"

"Leave concern for the Emperor to me, Korimizu. Rest assured I shall do whatever must be done. Go now."

Korimizu lingered a moment longer, a sad expression on his young face. Then he bowed and left silently.

Daimigi watched his young son hurry through the snowy garden, his green robe billowing behind him. *He is a spring leaf blown about by gusts of winter. Another leaf on the Fujiwara tree. And I am but the topmost leaf, equally vulnerable to autumn breezes. Or summer winds.*

Daimigi ordered a servant to bring in a kicho, and he waited.

It was not long before the Chancellor saw Kitsune coming through the garden. She walked briskly, now and then carelessly allowing her pretty face to show above the large fan she carried. *Such inelegant behavior! How can she expect to become part of our family and act so?* He heard her enter through the shoji behind the kicho and settle herself. *The screen is hardly necessary with what she has allowed me to see already.*

"You wished to speak to me, My Lord?"

"Ah, Kitsune-san! Why I was only just saying to Korimizu how it had been such a long time since I last spoke to you, and what a pleasure it would be to talk with you again. Now here you are. It is kind of you to indulge an aging man's whims so quickly."

"Oh, but I am honored to do so, My Lord. I, too, have missed our conversations. So much seems to have changed in the past few weeks."

Daimigi noted a trace of melancholy in her voice. "And how are things with you these days? Are your accommodations to your liking? Do you have everything you need? If you require anything, you know you need only ask."

"Oh, no. Everything is quite lovely."

"And how is Kazenatsu? I fear I have not seen him much of late."

"Truly? I thought he had seen you the other night."

"Eh? Well, yes, but that was family business. We have not had a chance to be social. Tell me, is he treating you well?"

There was a slight pause before she replied. "Oh, yes. Quite well."

"Are you certain? I would hate to think that my son would be mistreating you in any way. You know you are considered one of our family. You are quite important to us. Please feel free to confide in me as though I were your own father."

"Well, Kazenatsu has seemed ... a bit preoccupied lately."

"Preoccupied? What could possibly be so distracting that he could ignore such a lovely one as you?"

Kitsune giggled. "My Lord, you are too kind."

Indeed, thought Daimigi. "I realize, of course, that his position causes him to be busy with affairs of state. Korimizu tells me Kazenatsu had to travel to the Kamo Shrine today to give offerings, for example."

"Kamo Shrine? Korimizu must have been mistaken, my lord, Kazenatsu has gone to the Iwashimazu Shrine of Hachiman."

"Hachiman?" Daimigi endeavored to keep his voice even. "What would Kazenatsu wish to ask of the God of War, and patron of the Minamoto clan?"

"It is part of his ... preoccupation, My Lord. Several nights ago he told me he had a vivid dream. Hachiman appeared to him in the form of a warrior prince with intense eyes and a rope around his neck. Kazenatsu said Hachiman told him of a way to solidify the power of the Fujiwara."

"Has he told you what this way is?"

"No, My Lord. But it required some sort of propitiation to Hachiman in exchange."

"In exchange for what?"

"I do not know, my lord. Kazenatsu has been most attentive to his pious duties. He just made a sizeable donation to the Tendai monastery on Mt. Hiei."

"Did he?" said the Chancellor in a low, dangerous voice.

"I hope you do not think him a spendthrift, My Lord. He said it was to further his dream. Surely that is in your interest also, is it not? My Lord?"

But Daimigi was too angry to speak. *My own son.*

"Please, you musn't think—He intends no harm by it! Oh, pay no attention to my foolish words! They are meaningless!"

"They mean, I fear, a great deal."

"No! You must not take it that way, My Lord! You would not punish Kazenatsu for the looseness of my tongue, would you? There could be no other reason for you—"

"Silence, woman! You have said enough! Leave me."

"Please . . ."

"Go!" Daimigi heard her sob and the rustle of her robes as she opened and closed the shoji. Looking out at the garden, he saw her run across the snow, weeping. As she ran, her scarlet mantle fell from her shoulders onto the path, bright red upon pure white. *Like blood in the snow. Soon it may be—Fujiwara blood.* With a sigh, Daimigi took paper and brush, and began to write the order for the immediate arrest of Fujiwara no Kazenatsu.

Frozen River

Lying still on silk cushions on his dais, the Emperor watched as the old Shinto priest entered. *So. Is it the Hour of the Snake again?* thought the Emperor.

It is, said the spirit's voice within him.

How many days has it been that he has come in at this time?

Many, replied the voice.

The priest, in white vestments and hat, bowed slowly and respectfully towards the dais. Then he brought forward bowls of rice and vegetables, as he had done every day since the Emperor had become possessed.

The Emperor felt the spirit take command of his arms and take the food bowls from the aged priest. Desperately, the Emperor tried to move his mouth, trying to speak to the priest. But the spirit held back his tongue, and his jaw waggled uselessly. The priest looked sadly at the Emperor and turned away, shaking his head.

The Emperor closed his eyes and fell back against the pillows, sighing.

Have you not yet learned that you cannot defy me? said the spirit.

Why do you torment me thus? thought the Emperor. *Why not kill me and be done with it?*

That would not suit my purpose. While you remain in this uncertain state, the strife between and within the powerful clans can fester and grow. You must remain thus until the turning of the year, when all will be frantic concerning the promotions. Then I shall do with you whatever will cause the most chaos among the Fujiwara. Rest assured, your wish shall be answered soon enough. When it comes time for me to leave your body, I shall gladly guide your soul to the gates of Hell.

The Emperor heard someone else enter and speak to the priest. Opening his eyes, the Emperor saw it was

Daimigi's young son, the General of the Guards. *So,
Korimizu. Your father has no doubt sent you to check on my
condition. He is running things smoothly for me while I am
"indisposed," I take it?*

The Chancellor's regency is not as smooth as you think, said
the spirit within. *I have seen to that.*

The old priest left the room and Korimizu approached
the dais with an expression of sorrow and worry.

Need a better look, do you? the Emperor thought bitterly.
*Well, I am as I ever was. Powerless as usual, only now physically
as well as politically. I hope you haven't come to gloat. It would
be unbecoming in a scholar like you.*

But, to the Emperor's surprise, Korimizu's eyes red-
dened with tears. From somewhere he produced a brush
and paper and wrote what appeared to be a poem. Setting the paper respectfully beside the dais, Korimizu bowed
deeply. Then he rose and hastily departed.

May I read the poem? the Emperor asked the spirit.

Why not? It may prove to be amusing.

The Emperor reached over the edge of the dais and
picked up the paper. He read:

> To see the Heavens so obscured by clouds,
> If only tears could melt this frozen river.

Well, well, said the spirit, *it would appear one Fujiwara has
a loyal heart.*

The Emperor felt a sudden surge of gratitude and
affection for Korimizu. Then sorrow, knowing he could
never tell him. *Spirit, may I weep?*

No.

General Confession

Korimizu clumped along the veranda of the Household Minister's quarters, ignoring the soft touch of snowflakes on his cheek. Since the misfortunes of his two brothers, he had been given more family responsibilities. His father relied on him more than ever, and this disturbed him. *How can I follow his wishes, run his errands, when I feel what he is doing is wrong?* Korimizu wished he could go back to his books.

The young general stopped beside an elegantly carved set of shutters and rapped lightly. In a few moments he heard the rustling of silk as a waiting maid inside approached.

The lower half of the shutters opened a bit and the maid slid a cushion out to him, saying, "Who is it who is so kind as to visit the home of the Minister of the Imperial Household?"

Korimizu's spirits rose a little as he recognized the voice of the poet Shonasaki. He had admired her from a distance, and mostly by reputation. It pleased him to have the chance to speak with her. He knelt on the cushion and said, "It is I, Fujiwara no Korimizu. I bring a request from my father, the Chancellor, for Lord Echizen no Netsubo." Korimizu feared that he sounded too pompous, but he felt a need to impress Shonaski.

"I am most sorry, Korimizu-san, but the Lord Minister is unable to receive messages at this time. He is observing abstinence in preparation for the Day of Confession. But you may tell me His Excellency's request and I will see that it is passed on."

Korimizu sighed. It was a lie, of course. Netsubo was not known for great expressions of piety. *No doubt he is trying to avoid sticky questions from the Guard about Su K'an.*

Korimizu wondered if the lie on Shonasaki's tongue tasted as bitter to her as the ones he would have to tell.

"Please inform the Lord Minister that my father would like the painted screens and the statue of Kwannon set up in the Fujiwara Palace for the General Confession. His Majesty is . . . not feeling himself lately, and would prefer that such a demanding ceremony be handled by the Chancellor and high ministers. He felt it would be inauspicious to have screens depicting the horrors of Hell in the Seriyō Den when the wedding is so near. It might upset the young bride." *There. I've said it. Just as my father wanted.* Korimizu hated himself.

There was a pause and then Shonasaki replied, "I understand. I will give the request to a senior clerk who will see it done." Then she added, "We rather expected it."

Korimizu noted her sardonic tone and sympathized. *Yet I still must play the loyal son.* He wanted to stay in her company awhile longer, but needed desperately to change the subject. Korimizu asked, "Could I please hear one of your poems, Shonasaki-san? I have not heard your work since the uta-awase, and I would like to hear more."

Shonasaki paused again before replying. "I am very sorry, Korimizu-san. I have written nothing of quality since the contest. Things have been so sad here that I cannot bear to put my feelings on paper." Another pause, and then, "Please, Korimizu-san, you must know something. What is wrong with the Emperor? Why can we not see him? Is he ill? Or worse?"

Korimizu bowed his head and watched tiny snowflakes melting as they fell on the back of his pale hands. He tried to speak but could not. *I can't tell any more lies. Not to her.*

After long moments of silence, Shonasaki sighed and said, "I see. Is that the way of it, then? In that case, perhaps it is just as well that I am leaving the Court."

"What?" Korimizu snapped his head up and stared at the shutters as if his gaze could bore a hole through. "Leaving the Court?"

"Yes, Korimizu-san. Tomorrow morning."

"Oh." Korimizu felt regret well up within him and suddenly the air seemed colder. He shivered and sighed. "You are going home?"

"Not exactly. I have received word that there is a priest who knows the whereabouts of a . . . a dear friend of mine. I must seek him out so that I may find and join her."

"I see." *Yes, you are lucky, Shonasaki. You can leave this sadness to seek a friend. I am stuck here to tell lies to soothe my father's fears while the Emperor lies dying. You even get to see a priest. If I could talk to an outside priest, I'd . . .* An idea began to form in his mind.

"I am so sorry I have kept you sitting out in that inclement weather listening to my troubles," said Shonasaki. "I will go now to complete my packing, so that you may continue with your duties. I'm sure you are very busy these days."

Korimizu heard her silk kimonos rustle as she rose to go. "Wait!" he cried. "There is one more thing."

"Yes, Korimizu-san?"

The boy took a deep breath before he began. "Shonasaki-san, I have one last request of you. If I share with you the secret of what has befallen His Majesty, will you please take a message to your priest for me?"

Sunrise

Shonasaki hurried through the icy, dawn-lit streets of Heian Kyo. She was amazed at how busy they were, even at this early hour. Merchants, shop owners, innkeepers and artisans were opening for business, their breath steaming in the cold air. The fancy carriages of nobles and bureaucrats rumbled past, heading to offices or returning from lover's trysts. *Some of those carriage passengers at this moment are writing next-morning poems for the ladies they have just left.* Sighing, Shonasaki lifted the box of her belongings on her back and rushed on.

She wished she could have somehow borrowed one of Lord Netsubo's carriages. *Perhaps if I had been politer when I announced my resignation. Ah, well.* Though Shonasaki had put on drab clothing and hidden her hair and face beneath a large conical hat, she still felt uncomfortably exposed. The sooner she found the house she sought, the better. *But what will I tell the priest when I find him?* There was that strange, disturbing message the young Fujiwara had asked her to pass on. What had he possibly thought she could do? But she had promised to try.

After some searching, and awkward questioning of local residents, Shonasaki came to a small, run-down house. Cautiously she stood by the shutters and called out "Hello? Is anyone in?"

"Someone is in," replied a gruff voice. "Why does anyone care?"

"Please, I am searching for a priest."

"Does this look like a temple, woman? What makes you think there is a priest here?"

"If you please, I was told a priest named Takenoko was staying here. He knows the whereabouts of a lady I used to serve at the Palace."

"There is no one here anyone from the Palace should be concerned about."

Then a female voice came faintly from further in the house. "Shonasaki? Is that you?"

"Lady Uguisu! You are here too?!" Her heart leapt

with joy, and Shonasaki had to restrain herself from pulling open the shutters.

"Oh, please let her in, Kuma-san. She is a good friend."

Shonasaki heard someone grumble and the shutters were swung open. A somewhat disheveled man stood inside, eyeing Shonasaki cautiously. But she paid him little attention, giving him only a cursory bow as she hurried inside. She found Uguisu sitting by the hearth, and Shonasaki rushed to embrace her. "My Lady! Oh, you look so thin! Have you been treated well?"

"Oh, yes. Well enough. It is so good to see you, Shonasaki-san. But why have you come to find me? Were you banished from Court too?"

"No, I left by my own choice. I—oop, what's this?" Shonasaki felt something soft shift beneath one leg and she moved aside. With a disgruntled meow, a yellow cat crawled out from under her and stretched.

"Can this be . . . it is Hinata-san! Oh, I am so sorry, Hinata-san. I did not mean to be so rude. I am glad to see you, too."

The cat blinked at her and gave her hand a desultory lick.

A shoji slid aside and a woman who looked slightly familiar to Shonasaki sleepily entered the room. "Who is this, Uguisu?" said the woman. "Do we have yet another guest?"

"This is Shonasaki, Katte-san. She served me at Court."

"Ah," said Shonasaki, "You were the Lady of the Kitchens. I remember now. Everyone at Court wondered what had happened to you."

"Like you, I chose to leave."

There came rustling sounds from a dark corner of the room, and a young man with short hair sat up and yawned.

"Takenoko!" Kuma said, "Wake up! There is a lady from the Palace here to see you."

"Eh? What? Ah, Shonasaki-san. What brings you here?"

Suddenly Shonasaki was aware that there were men in the room who could see all three ladies clearly. She turned to Katte and said, "Excuse me, but have you no kicho for My Lady and yourself?"

"Fah!" said Katte. "I have had quite enough of kichos and other courtly things. I am now plain, poor Katte again. As for the men, Kuma is my husband, and Takenoko is a priest and a friend. I do not fear their seeing me. If Uguisu wishes, there is that screen there that she sleeps behind, but I do not think it becomes her at all. I am sorry, Shonasaki-san, if my hospitality seems poor to you, but this is not a wealthy household."

Feeling chastened, Shonasaki said, "I am sorry, Katte-san. I did not mean to seem demanding." She turned and opened the lid of her cedarwood box. She pulled out a silk bag that contained some gold and silver hair combs. Handing the bag to Katte, Shonasaki bowed and said, "To atone for my rudeness, and to offset whatever expense my presence may cause you, please accept these."

"Oh, no, I couldn't possibly!"

"Please. I shall not be needing them again."

Katte looked at Kuma who gave her a curt nod. Then she bowed, saying, "This unworthy one accepts your kind generosity, Shonasaki-san. Please feel welcome in our house."

Shonasaki bowed in return and took from the box a plain comb of tortoise shell with which she began to comb Uguisu's hair. "You are fortunate in a way, My Ladies, to have left the Palace so soon. It has become so sad. That is why I left—Oh, Takenoko! The message for you! I was so pleased to see Uguisu-san, I nearly forgot. It was very strange. Yesterday the Chancellor's young son Korimizu approached me. He had heard me say I would be seeing a priest and wished me to pass on a message. He said His Majesty the Emperor, whom no one in the Palace has seen for many days, is very ill. The Chinese lady has disappeared also. Korimizu believes His Majesty is possessed by some evil spirit, but his father will let only the family priest near him and will not allow an exorcism. Korimizu begged me to ask you to somehow help but I don't see what you can do."

Uguisu's brows shot up and she clutched the hem of her kimonos until her knuckles were white. "The eyes!" she whispered fiercely. "No wonder she looked at me that way. And now she has him and all I did to save him was useless! It is all my fault!"

"Please, what are you talking about, My Lady?"

Uguisu grabbed Shonasaki's sleeve. "The evil spirit! Su K'an was my guardian kami and she's going to kill all the Fujiwara and the Emperor and make her son the new Emperor! I tried to warn them but they didn't understand! Oh, I should have died before I was born!" Uguisu began to weep.

Shonasaki put her arm around Uguisu's shoulders. "What are you saying, My Lady? How do you know this? Yes, I remember you were worried about evil spirits, but why are they your fault?"

Tearfully, Uguisu recounted the story of how she was born to a family of witches, and how her guardian kami guided her to be an instrument of her family's revenge.

Shonasaki sucked in her breath through her teeth. "Ai, that is a terrible tale, Uguisu-san."

Quietly, Takenoko approached and knelt before them. "Truly, your karma has placed heavy burdens on you. But I cannot believe your past lives were so evil as to cause you to deserve such sorrow. Perhaps the Almighty Amida is testing you, trying your soul for greater glory to come. It is difficult to go against the wishes of one's family to do what is right. Surely you will not be blamed for this."

Stroking Uguisu's hair, Shonasaki murmured, "Korimizu also defied his family to tell me of the Emperor's condition and ask for help. And his betrayal no doubt took as much courage as yours. If only we could somehow do as he asked."

"But if this spirit is so clever and powerful that she can possess our Emperor," said Katte, "how could anyone defeat her? Who is more powerful than the Emperor himself?"

"The head of the Fujiwara," Kuma said sardonically.

Shonasaki narrowed her eyes at him. "That's not what she meant. Even so, the Chancellor would not help us. Korimizu said he forbade all help to the Emperor in order to keep events under his control."

"He is a fool!" Uguisu cried, striking the floor with her fist. "They will all be killed!"

"Come, now," said Kuma, "how can you be sure of that?"

"The Chancellor's son, Hidoi, is already dead. He drowned, but the guards say that he seemed mad or possessed as he ran towards the river. Kazenatsu has disappeared and is rumored to have committed some grave error for which he awaits punishment. Perhaps the killing of the Fujiwara has begun already."

Takenoko said softly, "Amidabha, bodhisattva, the Great Kami—"

"Are you praying, Takenoko-san?" asked Shonasaki.

"No, I was merely thinking of who was powerful enough to help the Emperor."

Katte said, "Isn't there one of the Great Kami who specifically looks after his Majesty?"

"Amaterasu," Uguisu whispered.

The cat Hinata, who had been curled up asleep by the hearth, raised her head and pricked forward her ears.

"Yes," said Takenoko, "Amaterasu is the Great Ancestress of all our emperors as well as the Kami of the Sun. She would be the one looking after him."

"Then why doesn't she help him?" asked Katte.

"Asking why a kami does or does not aid one is like asking why the wind blows," said Takenoko.

"Perhaps she doesn't approve of this Emperor," said Kuma, "and she doesn't care what happens to him."

"That cannot be true!" said Uguisu. "The Emperor is good and kind! One cannot help but love him! Amaterasu could not possibly find him worthy of such treatment."

Shonasaki noticed Takenoko staring at Uguisu, and she wondered why his expression was sad. "Perhaps," she said tentatively, "Amaterasu does not know."

"How could that be?" scoffed Kuma. "She is Kami of the Sun and can see everything."

"Not everything is done in daylight," said Takenoko, "and much happens beneath the shelter of roofs."

"And," Shonasaki added, "her shintai, the Sacred Mirror, has been locked in the Imperial Shrine. If no one has opened the altar to speak to it, she would not be informed."

"Then we must tell her!" cried Uguisu.

"That is foolishness," said Kuma. "You can't just walk into the Imperial Shrine and ask to speak to the Sacred Mirror."

"There must be some other way," said Uguisu.

The cat Hinata got up and padded to Uguisu's side. "Mrow?" she said.

"Not now, Hinata-san," said Uguisu. "Takenoko, you are a priest. Is there nothing you can do?"

"I am a Buddhist priest, and the kami are the province of Shinto."

Hinata trotted over to Takenoko and put her face close to his. "Mrrrow?" she said. Takenoko gently pushed her aside.

"Well," said Kuma, "perhaps when you summon Amaterasu you can convert her to Buddhism."

Takenoko grimaced. "Well, I suppose it hurts nothing to attempt summoning. Certainly our cause is good. Now, what do we need? If her sacred shintai is a mirror, then a mirror should be part of the ritual."

"I have a mirror!" said Shonasaki. She pulled her box of possessions to her side and took off the lid.

Hinata came running over. "Mrow!" she cried, and gently struck Shonasaki's cheek with her paw.

"No, I cannot play with you now, Hinata-san. This is important."

"Shall I take the cat outside?" said Kuma.

"That would be very kind of you, Kuma-san."

But as Kuma grabbed for the cat, Hinata leaped away and ran to the other side of the room.

Shonasaki pulled out of the box a bundle of red and purple figured silk. Unwrapping the silk, she produced a small bronze mirror. "Now what?"

Kuma grunted in exasperation as he continued to chase Hinata.

"Place the mirror in a beam of sunlight; over there should do. I will get some incense and a prayer-scroll."

Shonasaki propped the mirror against a wall in the midst of a sunbeam. But suddenly Hinata dashed over and sat directly in front of the mirror. Shonasaki sighed and began to move the cat, when bright golden light blazed out of the mirror. She had to cover her eyes, the light hurt so.

Katte and Kuma said, "What is it? What is happening?"

A voice smooth as honey said, "If you please, I would prefer that the cat remain."

The blaze of light dimmed to a golden glow, and Shonasaki slowly uncovered her eyes. Hinata sat before the mirror as before. But instead of a cat's reflection in the mirror, there was a beautiful woman's face, shining like the sun.

"Amaterasu!" Takenoko whispered, and he bowed very low.

"It is pleasing to be recognized," came the beautiful voice from the mirror, "even by one of a foreign faith."

Shonasaki gasped and bowed also, followed quickly by Kuma, Katte and Uguisu.

"Great Mother of the Sun," said Shonasaki, "I am honored . . . I mean, how did you come to be in my mirror before we even called to you?"

Bright laughter spilled from the mirror. "Hinata is my avatar—a part of me is with her, you might say. It is through her that I may appear in your mirror. It is through her that I would watch what happened at the Palace."

Kuma rubbed his chin. "Great Amaterasu, I mean no disrespect, but as you are one of the highest kami in our land, why couldn't you help the Emperor? He is your descendant, after all. Why could you not have prevented this calamity?"

"Please forgive this inattentive one, wise Kuma. It is surely a grave failing that I let things deteriorate so that no one thought to consult me until now. And my avatar, Hinata, was banished from the palace, so she could not help."

Kuma winced and bowed.

"Great Amaterasu," said Uguisu, "now that you have learned of the Emperor's plight, you will help him, won't you?"

"I will do what I can, child of the Earth. But although I am called a Great Kami, I am still only a kami. There is much I cannot do. I will need the help of all of you."

"But Amaterasu," said Shonasaki, "all of us are unable to return to the Palace, for one reason or another. We are as helpless as you."

"Not so, Lady of Poems. For between the five of you there exists the knowledge and the skill to achieve all that is necessary in unorthodox ways."

"What does she mean?" asked Takenoko.

"She means we can sneak in," said Kuma. "And she is right. I know all the movements of the palace guards. You, Takenoko, know the palace grounds better than anyone."

"So we could get in," said Takenoko. "But then what?"

"Then you, Takenoko, must perform the exorcism to free the Emperor," said Amaterasu.

"Me? But . . . but I haven't the skill yet! I should not be entrusted with such a task. Let me ask my master, who is—"

"Who is old, Takenoko. And the spirit we must fight is very powerful. Your master would not survive the ordeal long enough to complete his work. You are young and strong."

"I see. But I still do not know all I should."

"You will have time to prepare. The best time to challenge the spirit will be the early morning of the first day of the New Year. During this time, all spirits visiting this earth are called back to the Other World from which they come. If the spirit possesses a body, it will anchor her to this Earth and she can resist the call. But if she can be coaxed or forced from the body in the Hour of the Hare, just before sunrise, then she will have no anchor and must answer the call of Emma-O, Lord of the Dead."

"But New Year's Day is a full month away," said Shonasaki. "What if Our Majesty should die before then?"

"I think he will not," said Amaterasu. "The spirit wishes the destruction of the Fujiwara more than the death of the Emperor. She will achieve this best by keeping His Majesty's fate uncertain until the New Year promotions."

"And His Majesty will have another month to suffer," Uguisu said sadly.

"That is very much to be regretted," said Amaterasu. "But it is the only time we will have a chance of success."

"Well, that seems straightforward enough," said Kuma. "Takenoko and I should be able to manage. But what reason could there be to involve the ladies in this dangerous task? Surely Takenoko and I could do this alone."

"No, no," said Amaterasu, "they are very important. Uguisu must play the flute for him."

"But my flute is broken, Great Mother of the Sun," said Uguisu. "And even if it were not, what good would my music do?"

"I will provide you with another flute. And your music is vital. The Emperor's spirit has no doubt been broken by your guardian kami. You must, through your music, give him hope . . . give him a reason to live. The exorcism will not succeed without his efforts as well. He must have the inner strength, courage and motivation to drive the spirit from within. Your music will give him this."

"But," said Kuma, "there is no reason Katte should go."

"She knows the Palace as well as Takenoko, and her knowledge will be needed."

"What of me?" asked Shonasaki. "Poems will be of no use to the Emperor."

"For Takenoko to perform an exorcism, he will need a medium—a human vessel into which he can transfer the troublesome spirit. This is the most dangerous task of all, for the spirit will be angry and may try to harm you. You must use your cleverness to distract and weaken her further so that Takenoko's work may succeed. Will you do this?"

Shonasaki felt pride and fear mix within her. "I will do all I can for my Emperor and my Lady," she said at last.

"I am pleased," said Amaterasu.

"But exorcism with a medium will cause a great deal of noise," said Takenoko. "We will alert the Palace, and someone will try to stop us."

"Here is where your master may help. He must get word to the High Priestess of the Kamo Shrine, who is the Emperor's daughter. She, in turn, will inform the other shrines. All are naturally interested in participating in New Year's celebrations."

"But there will not be New Year's celebrations this year," said Shonasaki. "All priests save one are banned from the Palace."

"Yes," Amaterasu said calmly. "That is why they will help, never fear. Now there is one final thing I must ask. So that I may assist you in whatever way I may, you must take the Imperial Mirror from its resting place and bring it to the Emperor's chambers."

Takenoko's eyes went wide. "You mean we must desecrate the Imperial Shrine?"

A pale beam of sunlight came out of the mirror and touched the priest's forehead. "I shall forgive you."

Hinata yawned and blinked sleepily. "I am tiring my avatar," said Amaterasu, "and without her help I cannot remain in this shintai. Therefore I shall leave now. I will not speak to you again until my own Mirror is freed. My blessings are with all of you. With your courage, skill and cleverness we will not fail."

Slowly the light faded from the mirror, and Hinata curled up beside the box and went to sleep.

Katte, Kuma, Uguisu, Takenoko and Shonasaki all gathered together around the hearth, and were silent some moments. "Can we truly accomplish this?" said Takenoko.

"We must," said Uguisu.

"Of course we can," scoffed Kuma.

"There are only five of us," Katte said.

Shonasaki stared into the glowing coals in the hearth and said,

"It took but two to create all the world,
Who can say what five yet might accomplish?"

Spring

Curious how the air
Crisp on this mountain road
Tastes of plums—ah! Dawn.
                    —Bashō

DEVIL DANCE

IN THE DARK OF midnight, two palace guards stood shivering and stamping by the Eastern gate of the Greater Imperial Palace. "It seems strange, this silence," said one guard. "Particularly for the night before New Year's Day. There should at least be a Demon Chase. Some of our company should be twanging their bowstrings by now. Say, do you remember last year when—what's that?"

In the moonlight, the guard could make out the forms of several bald-headed, dark-robed monks approaching the gate in silence.

"Who goes there!"

The monks stopped and an old one at the front intoned, "We are the priests of Ninna-Ji. It is the New Year, and we have come to drive the demons and evil spirits from the Palace."

"You may not enter," said the guard. "It is the order of His Excellency the Chancellor, representing the wishes of the Emperor. No more priests are needed in the Palace."

"Far be it from us to defy an imperial order," said the old monk dryly. "In that case, we shall conduct our services outside." And the monks turned and began to chant loudly, marching single file around the palace wall. "Wait!" called the guard. "There must be silence! You cannot do this!" He was about to run after them when the other guard shouted, "Here come some more!" Walking through the snow towards the gate was another, larger group of monks. "Who are you?"

"We are the priests of Chisoku In. It is the New Year and—"

"We know what the date is! And you may not enter!"

"In that case, we will join our brothers in their services." And this group of monks followed after the priests of Ninna-ji, chanting loudly the Lotus Sutra.

Exasperated, the guard determined to collar one of the priests, while the other guard dashed off to get help. But then he saw yet another group approaching, all dressed in white robes and led by someone in a sedan chair.

"We are the priests from the Kamo Shrine," said a female voice from inside the sedan. "And as it is my father's wish that we do not enter, we shall join our brothers in their services."

The guard gaped after them as they joined the procession around the perimeter, banging on gongs and rattles. He knew the woman must be the High Priestess, the eldest daughter of the Emperor. He wished he could have caught a glimpse of her, and watched with admiration the shy and nervous vestal girls who shuffled daintily after her sedan.

Suddenly he heard a cough behind him and he jumped around. Standing just behind him were many monks who were nearly invisible in their black robes. Moonlight glinted off the sword hilts at their sides and they stood with an assured calm that seemed almost threatening. "We are the Tendai priests of Mount Hiei," said the foremost one in a voice smooth as a tachi blade.

The guard gulped, all too aware of the reputation of the infamous warrior monks of Hieizan. Quickly, he stepped back. "Yes, by all means, feel free to follow your brothers in their services."

And the warrior monks joined in the line of marching priests, chanting as loud as the rest.

The guard sat by the gate, knowing now he dared not interfere. Holding his head between his hands, he thought, *Well, there goes my promotion.*

Kuma and Takenoko crouched low in the ditch just inside the city's north wall. Each wore white trousers and red over-jackets similar to the palace guard uniform. Katte had made them from her old kimonos and some cloth she had been able to scrounge from a neighboring merchant. To disguise Takenoko's short hair, Katte had fashioned a fake helmet from an old wooden rice bowl and some bamboo slats. Kuma was grateful this excursion was taking place at night—their disguises would never have withstood the light of day.

Across the broad avenue from where they hid was the low wall of the Imperial Palace compound. Just behind the wall, Kuma knew, were stationed two armed, and probably drunk, guardsmen.

Kuma peeked cautiously over the edge of the ditch, looking up and down the avenue. No one was wandering in their vicinity. *Revelers will still be at the mansions of friends,* Kuma reminded himself. He had heard that the Minister of the Left, a Minamoto, was throwing a particularly large banquet tonight.

Then, from off to the right came the sound of chanting. "Do we go now?" Takenoko asked anxiously.

"No. Wait."

They waited until the voices got louder and they could see the dark forms of the monks coming around the corner of the compound one block away. "Now!" said Kuma.

They left the ditch and rushed across the street to the wall. Kuma leapt onto it and looked down to see two guards, holding sake cups, looking up.

Thought so. "Hoy! You there! We've got trouble coming! Priests from Mount Hiei! Come out here and guard this wall."

"What! Hiei? Here?" The guardsmen scrambled in confusion in the snow before managing to clamber over the wall.

"Here they come," said Kuma, pointing down the street.

"Almighty Buddha, there's a lot of them!" said one guard.

"Hold fast," said Kuma. "My comrade and I will go bring reinforcements."

"Sir, don't leave us here!"

"Wouldn't we be more effective on the other side of the wall, sir?"

Kuma affixed the guardsman with a stern glare. "If they get past this wall, guardsman, there will be nothing left to protect! Understand?"

"Y-yes, sir!"

"Good." Kuma turned to Takenoko. "You come with me."

Takenoko gave a curt nod and followed Kuma over the wall. Behind them they heard:

"Who was that fellow?"

"Probably one of the Inner Palace men. You know how pompous those bastards are."

"Hai. Goddess of Mercy, what do we do now?"

Kuma chuckled to himself. He almost wished he could stay to hear more of the conversation as he and Takenoko rushed towards the Imperial Shrine. There was little cover on the white graveled grounds of the compound, so they made little attempt to hide. Kuma called out to the few guards they passed: "Warrior priests! Go to the walls! Defend the Palace!" This created confusion more than anything else, which also served their purpose.

Seeing the shrine ahead, Kuma and Takenoko hid behind a snowbank until the area was clear of guards. Then, fast as they could, they dashed through the torii, past the giant stone dogs, up to the stairs of the shrine. There, Kuma stopped. "Something's wrong."

"What is it?"

"Shhh!" Kuma crept up the steps to the large wooden doors of the main sanctuary. One of the doors was ajar, and faint candlelight spilled through the doorway. "Someone's in there."

"There shouldn't be any services until dawn!" said Takenoko.

"Shhh!" Kuma pushed the door open further and winced as it creaked. Slipping out of his shoes, he stepped inside, feeling Takenoko follow right behind. As quietly as possible, they moved through the two small antechambers to the inner sanctuary. There an old priest sat facing away from them, praying before the altar.

On the altar, between a sakaki branch and the purification wand sat a gold and sandalwood cabinet. Behind its locked doors lay the Imperial Sacred Mirror, the shintai of Amaterasu.

Suddenly, the priest sat upright. "Who is here?"

Kuma, not having expected this turn of events, felt his throat go dry.

The old priest turned around and regarded them angrily. "What do you want?"

Kuma finally managed to force out a bluff. "We saw the light in the shrine, Holy One. We were concerned and came to see what was happening. We had heard there was trouble at the walls."

The priest's eyes narrowed. "What section are you with?"

"The Middle Guards, Holy One."

"Then you should know that for the past month I have been in here every night, praying for our Emperor. Surely someone must have told you."

"No, no one did." *And that's truer than I care to admit.*

"Well now someone has. I assume you have not purified yourselves?"

As if we had time to stop in the lustration pavillion and bathe before coming in here! "No, Holy One."

"Then I suggest you leave before you desecrate this place any further."

Kuma frowned regretfully, but did not move. *We have come too far to let this old priest get in our way. But how do I get him to leave?*

"Is it your intention to offend the Great Kami, or do you have something else to say?" snapped the priest.

"Holy One, there are monks surrounding the Palace walls, conducting services against the Chancellor's orders. Perhaps if you were to speak to them, they might see reason and disperse."

"If they are followers of Buddha, they will pay little attention to me. And if they mean harm, I am safer here, where I may also protect our holiest relic."

Suddenly Takenoko brushed past Kuma. "Enough of these word games! Holy One, we have been sent by Amaterasu herself to save our Emperor. We need to take her shintai to him. Please open the altar."

The old priest's face contorted as if he might be about to laugh. "Sent you herself, did she?"

"Yes! You may open the altar and ask her."

"You mean open it so you may bash me and take the Sacred Mirror to satisfy your greed. Never!" The priest stood, his back against the altar. "You shall not touch this altar without spilling my blood."

Kuma anxiously fingered the sword hilt at his side. It brought very bad karma indeed to kill a priest . . . particularly in a shrine. *Takenoko, you fool!* "You are right, Takenoko. We are wasting too much precious time. Go join the others. Your part of the plan is more important."

"But we cannot succeed without the Mirror!"

"I will bring the Mirror myself shortly."

"You . . . You're not going to harm him, are you?"

"Go."

Takenoko hesitated, looking at Kuma, then the priest. Then he ran.

Kuma, hand on his sword hilt, took a step towards the stubborn priest.

Korimizu watched his father in the flickering lamplight. Daimigi showed no outward signs of tension as he sat writing the formal declarations of promotion, but Korimizu knew he was worried. Possibly even afraid.

"I am pleased for your company, Korimizu," the Chancellor said. "It is not as comfortable to do these things alone."

"The kami who kept me awake must have had your welfare in mind," said Korimizu.

His father rewarded him with a brief smile. "I hope some kami watches over at least one of us." Then his face became very serious. "The days ahead of us will be difficult, Korimizu. We shall need all the friendly assistance we can gather. You especially, because you are so young. Tell me, do you think any of the guards are loyal to you personally?"

"I don't know, father."

"I think you are wiser than that, Korimizu. The guards obey you because your father is the Chancellor. If something should happen to me, who will guard you from your own guards?"

Korimizu looked down at the floor. He felt uncomfortable with the way his father hinted lately at such dire changes. He could not sleep this night because visions of a dead Emperor, of a court in chaos, kept filling his head.

Suddenly Daimigi sat upright. In the distance, the chanting of monks could be heard. "What is that?"

"It sounds like . . . sutras, father!" Korimizu's heart suddenly filled with hope.

"Priests chanting when I have forbidden it?" Daimigi stood and glared at the blinds.

There came the pounding of feet down the corridor and the shoji slammed aside. A guard stood there bowing and breathing hard.

"Your Excellency, the palace is surrounded by priests. Hundreds of them! They insist on performing New Year's services."

"They must not be allowed to enter the Palace!"

"They seem content with remaining outside for the time being, My Lord, but . . ."

"But?"

"But some of them are from Mount Hiei."

Korimizu saw his father's eyes flash with anger. *No doubt he suspects new treachery.*

"Send the Thunder Guard to the walls and gates. Double the guards on the Seriyō Den. I shall go to the Eastern Gate myself to speak to these priests."

The guard bowed again and hurried off. Korimizu said, "Father, what—"

"Shh. There is no more time for talk, I'm afraid." Then with a rueful smile, the Chancellor added, "I'm sorry, my son. You should have been the one to give the orders. And I should be sending you to lead your men. But you are the only son I have left whom I may trust. I prefer that you remain here, safe."

"I understand, father." Korimizu bowed. He did not resent the usurpation of his duties this time. It gave him the chance to look into something much more important.

"Take care, my son," said the Chancellor. He took his long tachi sword from its rack and hung it from his belt. Then with a last nod to Korimizu he departed.

Korimizu sat very still for some moments after the shoji slid shut. As soon as he no longer heard his father's footsteps, he slipped out of the room and headed towards the Emperor's chambers.

Uguisu walked behind the priests of the Kamo Shrine, trying to pretend she was just another one of the temple's female attendants. Katte and Shonasaki walked on either side of her, doing the same. All three wore white kimonos over vermillion skirts, and each carried a large cypresswood fan.

Uguisu hardly felt the cold of the night. She was both afraid and excited. She also felt proud and relieved that she could finally do something good for her Emperor. *Perhaps in this small way I may atone for my sins to him.*

Hinata stuck her head out of Uguisu's sleeve and me-owed inquisitively. "Not yet," Uguisu whispered and gently pushed the cat's head back in.

"There it is," whispered Shonasaki. Uguisu looked up to see the great triple crossbeams of the Southern Gate just ahead. She almost wished to turn and run away. Instead she sighed and continued plodding forward, hop-ing that their friends from the Kamo Shrine could give them the chance they needed.

In front of the gate, their procession halted. The High Priestess called out from her covered chair to the guards who stood within the gate: "Come here! I would speak with you."

The bewildered and curious guards approached. Sud-denly all the other Kamo priests surrounded the guards, waving purification wands at them and blessing them in the name of Amaterasu. At this moment, the three ladies rushed past them through the gate, onto the palace grounds.

Creeping cautiously among the snowbanks, Uguisu hoped their white kimonos provided some camouflage against suspicious eyes.

"The Seriyō Den is this way," said Katte.

Uguisu felt lost. Despite the time she had lived at the Palace, she had actually seen very little of it. She thought it ironic that the one of them who had held the lowest rank was the one who knew the Palace best.

As they moved further within the grounds, they saw people running by, but no one paid them much attention. From the exclamations she could hear, Uguisu learned it

was the presence of priests from Mount Hiei that most
worried the guards and courtiers. Uguisu almost laughed.
Takenoko's master had only been able to convince a small
number of Hiei priests to come, and even those had been
skeptical of the project. But apparently those few were
enough.

"There it is!" whispered Katte.

Peeking over a snowbank, Uguisu saw the ornately
carved eaves of the Emperor's private quarters.

"Are you sure?" said Shonasaki.

"Yes, but . . . something's wrong. Kuma didn't say there
would be that many guards."

Poking her head up further, Uguisu saw three guards
sitting on the veranda, laughing and holding sake cups.
"What do we do?"

"We must try anyway, I suppose. If they are drunk
enough, we might slip past them."

So the three ladies, keeping low behind snowdrifts,
hurried towards the building. But the men on the veranda saw them and with surprising speed rushed over.
Uguisu felt one of them grab her sleeve and pull her
close. His breath reeked of sake as he said, "Well, look at
the fine rabbits we hunters have caught! Shall we stroke
their pretty white skins?"

"A fine winter harvest, indeed," said the guard who
had grabbed Shonasaki.

"Let me go!" cried Uguisu.

"Now, now . . . ladies should be more polite. You must
say, 'I'm so sorry, pretty please!' "

"If you please," said Katte to her captor, "we have
come to wait upon His Majesty. He will be most upset if
we don't arrive. You really ought to let us go."

The guards laughed. "We had heard His Majesty was
ill. If so, he cannot have much energy for fine ladies like

you. I don't see that he will blame us for detaining you a little longer."

"He wished to see us right away!" Shonasaki yelled, pummeling her captor's chest. Uguisu struggled. Suddenly Hinata leaped out of her sleeve and streaked off into the Seriyō Den.

"What was that?" said one guard.

Uguisu's guard said, "Our lady here brought a pet kitty, but our love-play was too much for it. Shall I show you how I would like to be petted, pretty one?"

Uguisu continued to struggle, fearful that their plans would fail. She could not overpower the guard, nor could she talk reason into his besotted skull. *Amaterasu, what now?*

"Stop what you are doing!" commanded a tenor voice.

"Eh?" The guards grunted and all heads turned in the direction from which it came. On the veranda stood Korimizu, glaring down at them. Hinata stood beside him, her tail thrashing to and fro.

"Well, if it isn't the pipsqueak general!" said Uguisu's guard.

"These ladies are too old for you, lordling," said another, "you'd best leave them to experienced men like us."

"How dare you!" growled Korimizu. "I am your commander! Let them go at once or your positions are in peril!"

"Ai, the puppy is growing teeth."

"You will go and tell your papa on us, eh?"

"Besides, we are performing our lawful duty by preventing these ladies from disturbing His Majesty. We are following your father's orders."

After a pause, Korimizu said, "My father sent for these ladies to wait upon His Majesty. Do you dare interfere with the Chancellor's orders? If you do not let them go at once, I will see that you are all ronin before the sun rises!"

Another young guard stepped out of the shadows and said, "Do you need some help with these ruffians, my lord? Shall I go bring some others to deal with them? We can't have our court ladies subjected to such shameful, boorish behavior."

Uguisu recognized the voice. *It's Takenoko! But where's Kuma?*

Korimizu looked at the young guard a moment, then glowered at the other three. "Well?"

One by one, grumbling, the guards released the ladies. Uguisu gasped with relief and stumbled towards the steps leading to the Seriyō Den. Takenoko took her arm and helped her up. Korimizu also assisted her until she was inside, behind the blinds. Then they went to help the other ladies.

Uguisu sat in the gloom, trying to recover her breath. She heard a soft thump in a nearby room, and then a strange scrabbling sound approached her. She felt something soft rub against her and heard a muffled "Mrow."

Korimizu, Takenoko and the other two ladies came in, Takenoko also bearing a lantern. Shonasaki was leaning heavily on Korimizu, and he eased her gently to the floor.

"Thank you, My Lord. Your rescue was most timely."

"It was very strange," said Korimizu. "A cat came up to me and led me out to the veranda. There I heard your voice in distress and saw you and those men." Uguisu wondered why Korimizu was staring at Shonasaki so, then realized that the boy had probably not been this close to a woman since he was a babe. She smiled to herself and discreetly looked away.

Uguisu heard a thunk beside her and looked down.

There sat Hinata, looking impatient. In the cat's mouth was a scarlet cord, which was attached to a magnificent gold and cedarwood flute.

"Oh, were you the one making those mysterious noises?" Uguisu carefully took up the flute. "This is what you want me to play, is it?"

Korimizu looked at her and gasped. "That's Emperor Kammu's flute, Cloud Chaser! It is very ancient and . . . you're Uguisu! And that's Hinata! Both of you have been banished—"

Shonasaki turned and grasped Korimizu's sleeve. "Please, My Lord, be quiet a moment. I have brought these people at your request to help Our Majesty."

"Ah!" said Korimizu, "then it was you who brought all those priests! I am impressed and grateful, Shonasaki, but I do not know how we will bring them into the Palace. My father—"

"They aren't going to come inside, My Lord. They are there to distract the guards. The priest who will truly help is already inside." She pointed at Takenoko.

"This one is a priest?"

Takenoko smiled awkwardly. "It is so, My Lord."

Uguisu leaned towards Korimizu. "I am sorry, my lord, to bring our troublesome selves into your hands, but we are here at your request. Amaterasu herself has sent us to revive Our Majesty. Please trust her wisdom. Please help us."

Korimizu looked at Shonasaki, who said, "It is true, My Lord."

Korimizu sighed. "Lately it seems those most trustworthy have become treacherous, and the traitors become the ones to trust. Very well. Follow me."

But when they reached their destination, Uguisu's heart stopped a moment. Two very alert guards sat beside the shoji that led to the Emperor's sickroom. Korimizu strode up to them confidently. "My father has sent these women to wait upon His Majesty."

The guards gave them only a bored glance as they opened the shoji and let them through. As Takenoko passed, one guard said to the other, "Huh. They're recruiting them younger every day."

"Probably a Minamoto or a Taira," said the other. "They're always competing for early rank."

Uguisu crept cautiously behind Korimizu through what seemed to be a labryinth of screens. The faint light from the few lamps in the room was diffused by the silk and paper partitions, gloomy as a full moon behind clouds.

At last they gathered around the imperial dais. Uguisu gasped when she saw the Emperor, lying utterly still on the cushions. *How pale and thin he is!* Seeing his kind, elegant face once more, Uguisu felt tears come to her eyes. "I hope we are not too late."

"I think not," Takenoko said. He removed his guard's jacket and pulled sutra scrolls out of his robe. "You must play now, Uguisu. His Majesty must be awake and ready for his ordeal."

Katte looked around frantically. "Where is Kuma? You said he would be here!"

"Shhh. He was delayed at the shrine. He should be here soon."

"He is all right, isn't he?"

"I believe so. He had only to convince the priest that we needed the Mirror."

"You mean you don't have the Mirror?" said Shonasaki. "How will we succeed without it?"

"We must start as best we can. Amida willing, he will bring it soon. Now, play, Uguisu."

Uguisu lifted the unfamiliar flute to her lips and tentatively tried a few notes, then a bit of a melody. She faltered as she became used to the instrument. Then she played an old saibara she had heard, "Cherry Blossom Girl." It seemed to express the joy of spring mornings and beautiful things that make life on this earth a time to be cherished, not merely endured. Uguisu did not know if this flute was magical, but she assumed it was chosen for her for a reason. So into the song she poured all the love she felt for the Emperor, all the joy she felt in his presence, all the yearning she felt for his recovery. Her heart leaped with hope when, after a few minutes, the still form on the dais stirred.

Kuma slowly drew his sword from its sheath.

The priest's eyes widened, but he lifted his chin defiantly. "You will not speak to Amaterasu?"

"I would not debase myself enough to bring a ruffian such as you to her attention."

"Then I have no choice." Kuma raised the long tachi blade and looked at it a moment. It had been handed down from his grandfather, who had been a commander under Shogun Sakanoue, in the service of Emperor Kammu, during the Great Barbarian Uprising. The sword had always been carried with honor. No shameful act had ever stained its blade.

"My life is a small price to pay to serve the Great Kami loyally."

"Silence, priest. You know nothing of the price to be paid." Kuma turned and went to a table along the side wall. There he picked up a bowl of water that had been left as an offering. Carefully, he poured the water over the blade of the sword. Then taking a piece of white silk that had also been an offering, he wiped the blade dry. Finally, he took another piece of white silk and wrapped it around the blade. Kuma turned and approached the priest again. Kneeling, Kuma placed the sword at the priest's feet. "Please accept this as an offering and speak to Amaterasu."

Slowly, the priest took up the sword, keeping his eyes fixed on Kuma. Ever so slowly, he placed the sword on the altar.

As soon as the blade touched the table, golden light blazed out through cracks in the cabinet. There came a rattle and banging on the altar doors as if something within was trying to get out.

With shaking hands, the priest opened the doors, and the shrine filled with sunlight. "Please, good servant," said Amaterasu from the Mirror, "allow this man to take what he needs. I have promised my aid so that we may save the Emperor."

But the priest flung himself prostrate on the floor, praying loudly and begging forgiveness.

Kuma stepped quickly forward, past the priest, and took from the altar the octagonal golden Mirror of Amaterasu. "Excuse me," he said to the Mirror and slipped it into his kimono. Without another word to the priest, Kuma turned and ran out of the shrine.

Ah, I hear music. The music of a flute, thought the Emperor.
It is only the wind and your sick imagination. Nothing more.
No. No! It is my Uguisu! She plays for me again.
It is merely some lord who has drunk too much New Year's sake.
Ah, then you admit it is a flute. If it is as you say, open my eyes and let me see for myself.
No. Tonight of all nights I cannot waste my energy to cater to your whims.
Not even to open my eyes? Well, at least you cannot stop up my ears. Over them you have no power.

I could give you nightmares such that you could not listen.

Ah, but that would take some of your precious energy. Tonight of all nights, you cannot risk that, eh? Let me open my eyes.

No!

You are afraid, spirit. I can feel it. Yes, it must be my Uguisu. No one else plays so beautifully. How she lifts my heart! Why did I ever send her away?

Because you are a fool.

I shall be a fool no longer.

Takenoko lit incense at the foot of the dais, then began to wave the wands of purification. Uguisu played the flute softly in the background. Katte held open the scrolls for Takenoko as he began to chant. As his master had taught him, Takenoko reached out with his mind and the power of his voice. Directing his power against the spirit in the Emperor, he felt as though he had caught a very big fish in a net. And the fish was resisting every attempt to pull it from the water.

He chanted on, and the Emperor began to struggle and thrash about on the dais. This gave Takenoko hope that the spirit was weakening and he chanted and waved the wands with even more effort. Takenoko felt his throat going dry. His arms ached. Sweat dripped on his face, despite the winter night chill. He began to gasp for breath between his words. It seemed to Takenoko that he could not continue much longer. Then, at the edge of his awareness, he heard the faint chanting of the priests outside the walls. He concentrated on their voices, and chanted in rhythm with them. He tried to take strength from them, and channel their fervor through his words. But something was not right. The priests outside were chanting a different sutra and their voices rose and fell in the wrong places, disrupting the rhythm with which he sang.

Takenoko's voice faltered and he began to lower his arms, ready to admit defeat.

Then Takenoko became aware of the tune Uguisu was playing. He had never heard it before, but the melody rose and fell in stately tones ... and the pattern felt similar to the sutra Takenoko had been reading. He swallowed and raised his arms again, softly chanting, testing to see if he could match the sutra to Uguisu's song. And it worked. The phrases fell together perfectly, and Takenoko felt his voice grow stronger and more confident. His heart was delighted that he could share his endeavor with her, that they could blend so well. He filled his voice with his joy.

Then Uguisu's tone began to change and for a moment Takenoko felt panic. *What is she doing? It was just beginning to work! She mustn't change it now!* But as he listened carefully, Takenoko realized her song had not actually changed. Uguisu was adding complexity to the melody, while retaining the rhythm ... but the extra notes followed a different pattern that somehow blended with the first. Something about the new pattern felt familiar to Takenoko. *The chant of the monks outside!* Takenoko concentrated on his chant once more, allowing Uguisu to blend the two chants in the music of her flute.

Like the silken cord that binds the slats of armor, Uguisu's tune wove the voices together. Takenoko felt the power in the voices build and grow stronger. He suddenly felt a surge of power, and his strength felt directed, more coherent. It was as if his stream of words became the Sword of Fudo, the Curer of Madness, with which he could thrust at the spirit.

The Emperor writhed more violently on his cushions. Takenoko sent his voice higher in pitch and volume, feeling as though it was soaring to Heaven, to reach the ears of the Amida Himself. He felt dizzy and saw fuzzy dots dancing before his eyes. The dots gathered together to become a vision—the bodhisattva Aizen-myo, whose statue he had seen on the road to his temple—dancing above the Emperor's dais. The bodhisattva sang a poem with the tune of Uguisu's flute:

"Has the tadpole finally found his legs?
See how he leaps upon the path of Heaven!"

And Takenoko chanted joyously, not to be blended with Uguisu, but for the sheer pleasure of watching the bodhisattva dance.

Then Takenoko felt something snap, and the Emperor sat bolt upright. The Emperor's mouth opened wide, and there issued from it a streaming gray mass, neither liquid nor smoke. More and more poured out of the Emperor and formed into a column over the dais. The Emperor fell heavily back onto his cushions as the column formed a face . . . the face of an old woman.

"Stop!" shrieked the spirit. "I can scarcely think with all this noise!"

"We will gladly stop," said Takenoko, "when you heed the call of the Lord Emma-O and leave this world."

"The Lord's call is not so compelling, yet. And I have much to do before I depart. You may think you have won, little monk," the spirit rasped. "But I assure you, greater battles await you." The face and the column melted back into formlessness and suddenly streamed towards Takenoko. Instinctively he closed his eyes and began again to chant. He felt a wave of coldness pass over him. Then he heard, behind him, Shonasaki scream and fall to the floor.

*   *   *

Kuma came up to the Seriyō Den, running as fast as he could. To the three clearly drunk guards outside he yelled, "I've an important message for His Majesty."

"Go ahead," said one of the guards, waving him on. "Everyone seems to want to see him tonight. He must be having a party."

Kuma nodded and dashed up the steps and down the long corridor. He stopped at the two guards at the shoji. "I have an urgent message for His Majesty."

"He is holding services," said one guard, "and cannot be disturbed. Can't you hear the chanting? Give us your message and we will tell him later."

"It cannot wait!" said Kuma.

"One moment, you look familiar. Weren't you once a lieutenant? Yes, the one involved in that scandal with the noblewoman. I heard you deserted and she disappeared."

Kuma scowled and reached for his sword, only to remember he had left it at the shrine. *If I deny their accusation, I might get away with a bluff and escape. But then I couldn't get the Mirror to His Majesty.*

The shoji slid open and Korimizu's head popped out. "What's going on out here? We need quiet for the services."

Kuma felt his stomach sink as he saw the young general who had sullied his name. There would be no escape now.

"Are you the one with the Mirror?" Korimizu asked.

So. Takenoko or the others have been caught too and have told the story. We have failed and the Emperor is doomed. There is no point in lying now. Kuma nodded.

"Well don't just stand there!" said Korimizu. "Hurry up and get in here! They need you!"

Shonasaki had not expected the possession to feel so cold, so intense. Yet she steeled her mind and thought, *I am ready for you.*

Are you, little poem painter? Is that not fear rippling down your spine? You will have much more to fear once I truly begin.

But you cannot begin, where there is no beginning. You cannot possess the mind you cannot catch. And Shonasaki sent her mind to that private place that was the wellspring of her art. She imagined herself running freely over meadows that were full of spring flowers. But the spirit caught up to her, and turned the grass to fire.

. . . Which Shonasaki turned to bright red plum blossoms.

. . . Which were turned into great, stinging red ants.

. . . Which she turned into children in bright scarlet robes.

. . . Which were turned into horrible tengu demons.

. . . Which became a flock of elegant cranes.

. . . Which became spears in the hands of fierce horsemen.

. . . Which became the surf of a beautiful ocean.

. . . But one wave grew huge and dark, threatening to drown Shonasaki.

. . . But she solidified it into Mount Fuji-san, tall and unmovable.

. . . But the spirit caused the mountain to grow and spread into an enormous dark cloud that blotted out all light. Shonasaki felt blinded, suffocated. There were no images to work with, only darkness. Shonasaki felt the beginnings of despair.

Suddenly, bright sunbeams stabbed through the black clouds, melting them away. Surrounded by golden warmth, she wondered if she had somehow died and been taken into one of the seven Heavens . . . perhaps reached Nirvana itself.

I regret that I do not have the power to offer you that fate, said Amaterasu's gentle voice. *You must earn that yourself. But I can protect you in this world, for now.*

Shonasaki felt the spirit's mind slip further and further away. She opened her eyes slowly and saw Korimizu hovering over her, gently smoothing her hair away from her face. Shonasaki gave him a little smile and he jerked his hand away and blushed. Then, slowly, he smiled in return.

Kuma gave a great sigh of relief. "So, it is done. We have succeeded." Reverently, Kuma put down the Mirror.

At the end of a passage of the sutra, Takenoko stopped his chanting and Katte set down his scroll and stepped away. But Kuma could see a joyous light remained in the young priest's eyes.

Kuma went to the imperial dais. There, he saw His Majesty the Emperor sitting up on the cushions, holding Uguisu's hand. Kuma bowed low. "My Lord, are you well?"

"I . . . appear to be," said His Majesty. "I owe many thanks to all of you. In time, no doubt I—"

Suddenly there came a clang from the other end of the room. The Octagonal Mirror went skidding over the wooden floor to a far corner. Between them and the Mirror stood Katte, a vicious snarl on her face. "This one was not prepared," she hissed. "This one I can possess easily. You have been very foolish."

"Katte-chan!" Kuma leaped to his feet and rushed at her.

But before he reached Katte, another grey column rose out of the floor in front of her. This resolved into a man with intense eyes and a rope around his neck. In his hand was a sword whose blade shimmered as if made from pure moonlight. "You will come no closer. I shall see that my mother succeeds."

"Nagaya-chan!" said the strange voice from Katte's mouth, "You were not to become involved in this! Do not endanger yourself—"

"Mother, we have waited too long for this! I will not permit these fools to defeat us!"

Kuma felt helpless without his sword. He could only watch as the ghost and Katte began to back away from the dais. He heard Takenoko try to chant again, but his voice cracked and faltered and fell silent.

Then the Emperor called out, "Here, Guardsman! Use this!"

Kuma turned and caught the object thrown at him. His mouth dropped open. It was the Emperor's own Sacred Imperial Sword. Kuma bowed deeply to the Emperor and drew the blade. Holding it, Kuma felt renewed strength and power: the power of all the Emperors, the might of all Japan. Smiling, he advanced on the ghost of Prince Nagaya.

Fear came into the ghost's eyes, but he held his sword steady. For long moments, the guardsman and the ghost stared at each other, measuring, watching, waiting. Kuma reached into the center of his strength, his muscles relaxed and ready. Then with an unworldly wail, Nagaya attacked and the fight began.

Uguisu tried to watch the fighters, but the swift movements of their dim forms were hard to follow in the gloom. All she could clearly see were showers of gold and silver sparks whenever the swords connected. She realized that she was holding her breath.

Suddenly she was distracted by a tugging at her sleeve. Looking down, she saw Hinata mewing and frantically running in circles. "What is it, Hinata-san?"

The cat turned and pawed against one of the screens near the dais. Uguisu looked around and realized she could not see Katte. *She's trying to get away!* Uguisu shoved hard as she could against the screen. It fell over onto the one behind it, which knocked over the screen behind, and so on, until the room was clear to the eastern blinds. Uguisu saw Katte creeping towards the blinds, turning to glare at Uguisu as her position was revealed. Uguisu tried to remember where Amaterasu's Mirror was.

Hinata ran to the near edge of the blinds where the drawstring was and meowed loudly. This time Uguisu caught the hint and rushed after her. Peeking outside, Uguisu suddenly understood, and fast as she could, pulled the blinds open.

In the clear, pale winter sky, to the east, the sun was rising.

Prince Nagaya looked around in surprise. In that moment Kuma brought his sword down in a slashing movement across the ghost's chest. Nagaya snarled and raised his sword to strike, then his mouth opened in shock as grey fluid oozed from the wound across his chest. He dropped his sword and moaned, clutching his chest as he settled towards the floor.

"The sword has the power to punish those who betray the clan of Yamato," said the Emperor.

As the spirit in Katte stared at the rising sun in surprise, Uguisu noticed a golden glinting against the wall. Uguisu dived for it, her hands closing around the edge of the Octagonal Mirror. She leaped up, holding the Mirror so that it caught the golden-pink rays of the morning sun and focused them on Katte's face.

The spirit squealed and raised her arm to block the light, eyes tightly shut. The grey mist flowed out of Katte, but to Uguisu's surprise, the spirit was smiling. "It is past the Hour of the Hare, and I am still on this earth!" the spirit said triumphantly. "I may now remain for another year, during which time I may yet achieve the revenge for which I hunger. You are all snapping puppies against a bear, and I assure you my claws are still very sharp."

"Then they shall be most useful in the underworld," said Amaterasu, rising out of her Mirror. She wore yellow and white robes of such brightness one could scarcely look at her. "You have been fooled, Evil One. It is only the Hour of the Ox. But it is my prerogative to choose when the sun may rise." Taking beams of dawn light, Amaterasu looped them around Prince Nagaya and his mother.

There came on the air a deep moan. It was barely audible, but the ghosts squirmed in their bonds. "It is the call of Emma-O!" said Nagaya. "Oh, he will give us a most harsh judgement when we return!"

"Fear not," said Amaterasu. "I did not intend to waste such powerful spirits as you on the pits of Hell. There is another who wishes your service." The ground rumbled and up from the floor came a wild-looking kami, with hair like a dragon's mane. He took hold of the bonds of sunlight of the two ghosts and laughed.

"I would like you to meet my brother," said Amaterasu. "His Impetuous Male Augustness, Susano no Mitoko. Though he was once a kami of storms, his current occupation is ruler of the underworld. It was he who gave me the idea of tricking you—in exchange, of course, for the service of your souls once you were caught. I understand there is much work to be done in his realm within the earth, and your stay will, no doubt, be long."

With a gleeful shout, Amaterasu's brother kami tugged on the bonds of sunlight and slid back down into the earth, dragging the two angry spirits with him.

For long moments there was only silence, as they all stared at the floor where the spirits had disappeared.

Then Katte sighed, becoming aware of herself again. She crossed the room to Kuma and laid her head against his shoulder. Kuma put one arm around her, but looked at Amaterasu with chagrin. The Sun Kami only gave them a brilliant smile. Uguisu realized that the Mirror had become heavy. Her arms ached. Slowly and reverently, Uguisu placed the Octagonal Mirror at Amaterasu's feet. Then Uguisu went to the Emperor and knelt beside him.

Amaterasu smiled at them also. "I owe you gratitude beyond measure, Uguisu. Because of your brave and loving heart, my descendant and his people are spared from Nagaya's wrath." Turning to the Emperor, she said, "She will be a very fine Empress."

The Emperor looked adoringly on Uguisu and took her hand. "I have known this for a long time."

Uguisu beamed with joy, but still found it difficult to meet his kind, loving eyes, and so she blushed and shyly looked away. She spared a guilty glance for Takenoko, wondering what he must think. But the young priest was not even looking at her. He was staring at nothing, a beatific smile on his face. Uguisu wondered at his expression, not knowing that before his eyes was the vision of a little god dancing.

Korimizu and Shonasaki were huddled together against the wall, staring wide-eyed at Amaterasu. The Sun Kami turned her beautiful golden face to them and said, "And I thank you, Korimizu, for your loyalty and courage. Without your unexpected assistance, our efforts might well have failed."

"It . . . it is a great honor," Korimizu managed to blurt out, and he bowed deeply.

The Emperor bowed reverently to Amaterasu. "I thank you, Great Ancestress, for your aid. And, of course, I thank all those present for their help as well."

Everyone bowed to the Emperor in return.

"It is my duty and my joy to look after my grandson's descendants," said Amaterasu.

Hinata jumped onto the Emperor's lap and licked his face.

"Well!" said the Emperor. "Didn't I banish you not long ago? No matter, you are pardoned. As are any of you who require it." He scratched Hinata's neck and she purred loudly.

Amaterasu said, "That is well. It will be good to have my avatar back in the Palace again. Then I need no longer bear the shame of negligence in my protection of you."

The Emperor looked at the cat, then at the Great Kami, an expression of chagrin spreading across his face.

"Your avatar?" He bowed again. "Please forgive this thoughtless, empty-headed one for the offense he has caused you. For sending away your little servant, and for denying you the attention and veneration that is your due."

Amaterasu inclined her head. "You are forgiven, grandson of many grandsons. In future, I shall try to remain closer to Hinata, so that I may better inform you in times of trouble. But you must promise me one thing."

"Yes?"

"Never say you have a cat who tells you everything. You may find your ministers maneuvering to become regents." Amaterasu smiled again and turned as if to go.

"Great Ancestress!"

"Yes?"

"What you have just said, I'm afraid, brings a question to my mind which I fear I must have answered. Please tell me why, O Great Mother of the Sun, you have allowed powerful clans like the Fujiwara to overpower your descendants. They have become mightier than Emperors and treat us like puppets. Is this truly looking after our welfare?"

Amaterasu sighed and lowered her head. "The question you ask, grandson of many grandsons, has an answer which, I fear, will be difficult for you to understand. It is by allowing these clans to take your political power that I am, indeed, looking after the welfare of my decendants."

"You are correct. I do not understand."

"Perhaps only a mother would understand my reasoning, but it is simple enough! Power is the most treasured and dangerous of all possessions. He who has it must be ever vigilant against those who covet it and would steal it from him."

"I know this all too well." said the Emperor.

"Then do you not see that if you were the possessor of greatest power, it would endanger your life and the lives of your family?"

"Yes, of course. But is that not why you should help us keep it?"

"Foolish one!" said the kami, looking near tears. "I do not care about your power! I care about *you!* And your children. And their children. And the stability and harmony the continuance of a royal line will give to this land. I do not wish you to become an iron-fisted ruler, who will only be toppled by another, bigger fist. You are the heart and soul of this empire, not its sword. You are its art, its poetry, its tradition. You are all that makes this land beautiful. I do not wish the Emperor of Japan to be thought a mountain to be conquered, or a prize to be taken. Instead you must be a treasure to be cherished, and loved by your people. Only in this way will my descendants, and yours, outlast the power-hungry. Only in this way will there be hope and stability for our people. Do you understand now?"

The Emperor bowed his head. "I shall try, Great Ancestress."

"That is good." Then a small smile appeared on her face. "You may take some solace in this: the Fujiwara will not last forever." She turned and stepped onto the Octagonal Mirror. Her image wavered and brightened until she turned into a golden column of pure sunlight. Then this sank into the Mirror and she was gone.

Official News

Chancellor Fujiwara no Daimigi watched the clusters of sleepy-eyed nobles as they filled the Great Hall of the Palace of Administration. He sat alone on the Ministerial Dais, feeling at once immensely powerful and extremely vulnerable. *Now comes the test of my own survival.*

He rubbed his face, trying very hard not to yawn. He had gotten no sleep, having been at the walls most of the night dealing with the priests. He did not know if his efforts had caused them to leave peaceably at dawn, or if that had been their plan all along. Daimigi could not help suspecting someone had set the whole thing up to distract him from working on the promotions. *Whoever it was almost succeeded.*

He felt fortunate that, at least this morning, he had the element of surprise. The strangely early dawn of this morning seemed to have caught everyone offguard. The Office of Divinations was still trying to determine what it meant. Daimigi chose to interpret it as a sign that he, too, should move sooner than expected.

When the hall seemed full enough, Daimigi clapped his

hands for silence. Then he bowed to the assembly, noting carefully the depth of their bows to him.

"A pleasant and prosperous New Year to all of you. I wish this could be like any joyous reception held on this first morning of the year. But I fear very serious matters are before us. Matters that must be dealt with immediately, lest they cause dangerous divisions and squabbles among us. Allow me, then, to tell you how matters stand.

"Our Glorious Imperial Majesty, as many of you know, lies gravely ill. Those who attend him say he may not remain with us long."

This brought much whispering and muttering from the floor. Daimigi slapped his baton of office on the dais to regain silence.

"I realize this news must bring tears to all eyes, still I wish you to know affairs of state are being carried out smoothly. The Emperor's nephew arrived, safely, some time ago and he is prepared to inherit the office. He has accepted my daughter as his wife and empress-to-be. I am currently looking into making the best arrangements for His Majesty's funeral."

"Aren't you being a bit premature?" said a voice from the doorway.

All heads turned, and then all heads simultaneously hit the floor.

Daimigi stared back in surprise.

"Good morning!" said the Emperor.

Epilogue

So thus we end our tale. How is that, esteemed reader? You say you wish to know the fates of all the characters? But they are only shadows, visions of a world long past . . . oh, very well.

Nikao finally did marry a silk merchant and they lived well, and they had many children to bring them joy (and support them in their old age).

Fujiwara no Kazenatsu was sent into exile in a far province. Kitsune went with him, although it is said she wept terribly at leaving the capital.

Shonasaki married Fujiwara no Korimizu. Do not look so surprised, esteemed reader. Yes, he was young, but that was often the way things were done in those days. It was a good match, for he admired her poetry, and she admired his scholarship. Korimizu was one of the few Fujiwara the Emperor would trust, and he grew to be a man of great importance. And it was said that his youth kept Shonasaki feeling young for many years.

As for Prince Nagaya and his mother ... well, you know we have many earthquakes in this land. Could it not be that as they toil in the underworld, they sometimes shake the islands with their rage?

Netsubo, Uguisu's father, was again made governor of Echizen province. It was a wealthy area, so it was not truly a punishment. But His Majesty, in his wisdom, thought Uguisu would be happier without her father near.

Takenoko, during his exorcism of the Emperor, had finally found his Path to Heaven, and he remained a monk. He lived to be old and wise, and much respected by those who knew him and his teaching.

Kuma and Katte, of course, were married. Katte wished nothing to do with the Palace, so the Emperor granted her wish to own a fine inn at the edge of town. Kuma also managed the inn and, at times, did special trusted assignments for the Emperor. There were days he dreamed again of being a guard, and life was not always smooth between him and Katte. But the love that grew from their shared troubles strengthened the bond between them and lasted until the winter of their lives.

Fujiwara no Daimigi remained Chancellor for several years more, despite the doubts of his kinsmen. To Daimigi's surprise, the Emperor himself wished to keep him in office. He even found His Majesty more agreeable to his advice. But Daimigi could never understand just what it was that caused the Emperor to look so smug.

Of course it was a glorious day when Uguisu was installed in the Palace as Empress. This time she did not deny the Emperor, and, before long, she bore him a son and heir, just as the divinators predicted. And when the Emperor finally acquiesced to the Fujiwara and retired, she went with him to a beautiful hillside palace retreat where they spent the rest of their days in peace and joy.

And as Amaterasu said, the Fujiwara did not last forever. Their overgrown bureaucracy became weak, as offices became more a matter of family standing than of ability. Stronger, more aggressive clans grew in the provinces, and within four centuries, the Fujiwara faded from power.

Great strife has visited this land for centuries since then. But as Amaterasu promised, through it all, her wisdom and her descendants have endured. And the Imperial Line of Japan has remained unbroken to this very day.

AFTERWORD

U*guisu: The Nightingale* is based upon the fairy tale classic "The Nightingale", written by the Danish author and playwright Hans Christian Andersen. The original tale was first published in 1843, along with "The Ugly Duckling" and "Sweethearts", and has since become one of Andersen's best known and loved works.

Here is a (much abbreviated) description of the plot of the original "Nightingale." Some time in the distant past in the land of China, there lived an Emperor in a beautiful palace. Everyone exclaimed how beautiful it was, particularly visitors, who would write about it in books . . . and what they noticed most of all was the nightingale. When the Emperor came upon such a book with such a description, he became distressed that he had not seen or heard such a bird. So he asked his very pompous gentleman-in-waiting why he had never heard of it and demanded that the bird be brought to him to sing that very evening.

So the gentleman and all the court went in search of the nightingale, and finally found a kitchenmaid who had heard it. The maid led the court out to the woods where they found the little grey bird sitting in a tree. The maid invited the nightingale to sing before the Emperor at court, and although the bird felt its song sounded better among the trees, it politely agreed.

When brought to the Emperor, the little bird sang so beautifully that tears rolled down the Emperor's cheeks.

When the bird was finished, the Emperor offered his gold slipper for the bird to wear around its neck. But the nightingale declined, saying the tears of the Emperor were its richest reward.

The bird became an insant sensation at court. Ladies would gurgle with water to imitate the nightingale. The bird had its own beautiful cage and footmen to take it for walks. But the nightingale did not much enjoy its situation.

Then one day a box arrived at the palace, and the Emperor believed it was another book about the nightingale. But instead the box contained an artificial clockwork nightingale, studded with diamonds and rubies—a gift from the Emperor of Japan. When wound up, the artificial bird could sing one of the nightingale's songs and dance on its perch.

The Emperor thought this was a marvelous gift, and everyone's first thought was that the real and clockwork birds should sing a duet together. But when they tried, the duet sounded awful, for the artificial bird always sang in the same particular way, while the real one always varied its tune. So the clockwork bird sang alone, and everyone made such an appreciative fuss over it that no one noticed the real bird fly away back to its woods. The court was so insulted when they learned that the real nightingale had left that they banished it from the kingdom.

Now the clockwork bird was given an official place on the left side of the Emperor's bed, to soothe him and sing him to sleep. The court made as much fuss over it as the real one, imitating it and writing books describing its wonders. And this went on for a year.

Then, one night, as the artificial bird was chirping away, something went *sproing!* inside it and it whirred to a stop. The court watchmaker was sent for, and he proclaimed that the bird was worn out and should be played as little as possible. This distressed all the court, and the Emperor became so sick at heart that he lay ill in his bed and they began to think of a successor.

In the dark of night, the Emperor awoke, feeling a weight on his chest. There sat Death, holding his royal crown and insignia. Demons peeked out from the hangings and they all jabbered at him. The Emperor cried out for music to drown their horrible words. He commanded the clockwork nightingale to sing, but it stood silent as ever and Death still sat on his chest. Then there came marvelous music from outside the Emperor's window. It was the real nightingale, come to bring the Emperor comfort and hope. The bird's fresh song drove the demons away, and even caused Death to give up the crown and insignia he held in order that the nightingale would sing more. Finally Death was so charmed by the nightingale that he flew out the window, and the Emperor was restored to health.

The Emperor was, of course, very grateful to the nightingale and begged it to come back and live in the palace. The bird explained that a palace was not a proper place for a nest, but the bird would come by whenever it wished and sing for the Emperor. The nightingale's one request was that he not tell anyone that he had a little bird who told him everything. Then the nightingale flew away and the attendants came into the imperial bedchamber, to be surprised by the Emperor who wished them a hearty "Good morning!"

Naturally, this outline captures little of Andersen's magical writing style, or the lovely details of the story. He pokes marvelous fun at bureaucrats and courtly types, and there is much wry humor amongst the beautiful descriptions. I can only heartily recommend that readers seek out a copy of the original and read it for themselves.

As to the origins of the story, Hans Christian Andersen would himself admit that many of his stories were based on incidents in his own fairy-tale-like, rags-to-riches life. Scholars examining his work like to point out Andersen's championing the real over the artificial, the heart over the cold intellect. But "The Nightingale" was closer to Andersen's heart in another way as well.

In his fortieth year, Andersen fell in love with a Swedish singer named Jenny Lind, who was also known as "The Swedish Nightingale." She came to sing for the King of Denmark that year, and he was so pleased with her music that he gave her a gift of diamonds. The parallel to the story should now be fairly clear. Other comparisons have been made between the pompous bureaucrats and the critics of Andersen's works, and the fact that the Danish public generally preferred light Italian comic opera to Jenny Lind's more restrained music. Alas, Jenny did not share Andersen's deep affections, though she was fond of him, and he lived out his life a bachelor. Still, we can be glad that their acquaintance proved to be the genesis of so charming a fairy tale as "The Nightingale".

The Nightingale is one of my favorite fairy tales, remembered fondly from my childhood, although I could not exactly say what its appeal for me is. Part of it is the exotic setting, China, as opposed to the traditional northern European setting. Part of it is the kindness and graciousness of the bird as compared to the silly pomposity of the people around it. Suffice to say, I loved the story, and it was the first one to pop into my mind when Terri Windling invited me to write a fantasy based on a well-known fairy tale.

Terri also stated that I could ring whatever changes on the tale I wished, and as the reader has no doubt noticed I rang quite a few.

First, the setting. I placed *Uguisu* in Japan because I happen to know more about, and be more interested in, Japanese history and culture than Chinese. And one period of Japanese history that intrigued me was the Heian period (approx. 750–1100 AD). During this time, Japan was largely at peace and the Imperial Court could devote itself to the pursuit of style and grace, particularly in poetry and literature. Unlike other times in Japanese history, women became noted for their literary skill. At the latter end of the Heian, Lady Murasaki Shikibu wrote *The Tale of Genji*, a historical novel that is still a classic. Her diary, and Sei Shonagon's *Pillow Book* (also from the same period) provided me with much of the background for *Uguisu*.

Also, the Heian period was a time of much court intrigue, with various great clans vying for power. The bureaucratic system, imported from China, was absorbed wholeheartedly into the Imperial government, allowing me to poke fun at it much as Andersen did.

In short, the fairy tale and the historical place and period seemed a perfect match, and I was quite pleased with the outcome (as was my editor, Terri). I can only hope that the result has been pleasing to the reader as well.

Kara Dalkey
Minneapolis, Minnesota
November 1987